Books by the Author

The Bridge
The Proselytizer
The Death and Life of Harry Goth
War Is Heaven!
Horn
Bishop's Progress

THE BRIDGE

THE BRIDGE

D. Keith Mano

DOUBLEDAY & COMPANY, INC.
GARDEN CITY, NEW YORK
1973

All the characters in this book are fictitious, and any resemblance to actual persons, living or dead, is purely coincidental.

Designed by Wilma Robin

ISBN: 0-385-02870-9
Library of Congress Catalog Card Number 72–96248
Copyright © 1973 by D. Keith Mano
All Rights Reserved
Printed in the United States of America
First Edition

This book is for Elizabeth McKee . . .
with gratitude for her patience and encouragement.

CONTENTS

PROLOGUE

AT THE CREST he could hear the first eee-thud, eee-thud of the mortars. In the rear seat Carol clapped her hands. The Model T's hood hesitated, then dipped, level. Oscar shifted, gave the engine relief. His palms bore bracelet tooth marks from the steering wheel: he had been lifting hopefully with shoulders and hands while they drove the steep incline. Eleanor, beside him on the wooden seat, leaned forward, placed her fingertips on the dashboard gently, a grace note, hands spread octave wide. Carol, behind Oscar, caressed the seven months of her pregnancy. She rubbed the opaque ball, depressing it, prodding it, as though there were discrete, erogenous parts. Juices of her excitement intrigued the fetus. It moved. Carol leaned sideways on the rear seat. She touched her twin sister's seven-month pregnancy. It was a tough muscle, contracted. Julie giggled: a whinny, an extraordinary sound blown through mouth and nostrils, an arcane call of their childhood. Eleanor made fists when she heard this, the joined cry of Oscar's other wives. She glared at him. Oscar didn't see. Though reluctantly, he too had been thrilled by the mortars' drumming, by the meshed tusks of piping, falling sound. Holiday memories, his family: Oscar touched the red armband, a tourniquet for his left biceps. It was an austere civilization; this was ceremony and entertainment.

Across a narrow river valley they saw the crater's southern wall. Its rim was somewhat lower than the crest; its foreshortened mouth inscribed a silver ellipse. Dust from two hundred explosions sifted up: the kinetic uncertainty of a dormant volcano. The Adirondacks cowered, molars on its false horizon line; they shimmered, appearing insubstantial through the dust, through the blue haze of factory smokestacks active even on the Feast of Eater. The Model T braked downward along a one-lane dirt road. Against the engine's catarrhal, masticating pulse, the far rumble seemed an inverse echo: reverberations louder than the sounds that had made them. The road hairpinned; tall conifer growth appeared on its verges. Oscar slowed. He saw the other black Model Ts, a slanting chain three hundred yards long to the bridge head. Each chassis a pedestal for its jiggling human busts.

"Bumper to bumper."

"We should have come yesterday."

"I was busy, Eleanor."

"We should have come yesterday. There's nothing left. I know it."

White/green insecticide sugared the cedar trunks: on the southwest, the side of the prevailing wind. Serrate branches sawed slowly, parting the still air's ivory bone. It was humid. The traffic had whisked up a great awning of dust. It shaded them as the Model T drove under; it fell into their sweat.

14

Julie and Carol were redheads; dust connected their russet freckles. They had no maternity dresses. Deerskin bodices had gradually been let out on thongs, Venus-flytrap jaws opening, as though their clothes, too, had conceived. Sweat of long wearing stained half circles under armpits, darker, lighter, the isobar chronicles of waves on sand. Their moccasins were black with body oil, pliant and comfortable, new animals living in them. Eleanor did not sweat. Her skins were carapaces that cracked; they did not learn the shape of her thin body. She wasn't pregnant.

The crater wall loomed now. Fifty yards ahead traffic passed over a poorly leveled culvert. Oscar watched torsos crest, bow, right themselves. Then Eleanor and he bowed; Julie and Carol on the high platform back seat exaggerated the jounce, whinnying: fun. Some families walked. Several rode bicycles, wrenching handlebars against the false direction given out by a stone, a root, a snake of soil erosion. He counted six abandoned cars. Tires were vulnerable; the technology of rubber processing had proved obdurate and subtle. Traffic halted. Oscar stood to wipe dust from the far side of his square windshield. The glass jiggled in its frame. Trapped bubble imperfections clotted and chewed transparency. All new mirrors distorted. No one, Oscar thought, could exactly know his own face. He sat.

"They're all the same." The heavy chestnut braid flicked against Eleanor's shoulder. It was knotted hard, glossy: it could disgust him, arouse him. Eleanor's arms were wrapped against her chest. "I hate it. The same car. The same color." She pointed toward the bridge. "It's a nightmare."

15

"Don't start, for Priest's sake." Oscar let the clutch in. "I had that up to here yesterday. It's the best we can do."

"I saw that car book in your office. There were nice cars. Like cats. Not like coffins. This is a coffin."

"The Council decided and for once the Council was right. Ford's Model T is the most efficient, the simplest form of transportation ever invented." The image of Priest toppled from its magnetic grip on the dashboard. Oscar reset it. "Look, dearest. Let me explain again. For the first time in man's history, scientific knowledge is two hundred years ahead of technology. I can tell you how to build a supersonic jet plane. I can tell you how to make Mnemycin and Planktil. But I haven't got the tools." Eleanor jerked her head back by the braid; the skin of her scalp moved, lifting eyebrows. Her thumb plucked at the deerskin bodice.

"And these skins. I hate them most of all. I hate the feel of them."

"Please. There's no sense bitching about it. This is a holiday. Let's not spoil things." Oscar rapped the horn button; there was no sound. He blew breath through fattened cheeks. "I get this every month on the Ecotech committee. I'm sick of arguing priorities."

Sick. Sick. He spoke English well, exactly as the Eastern School of Eco-phonologists advocated: pronunciation standards based on the New York "Rosetta" tape. Yet there was no suppleness; it was an academic symbol code. Sometimes, dreaming, he sang growls, shrieked: in the morning his chin was tacky with drool. Oscar envied, feared the young Appalachia savages that Eleanor taught in speech therapy. Their evolved speech was of groans and clacking yips, set behind the mouth. Lips did not move; their faces were expressionless as dog muzzles. Sick of arguing, he whispered. Oscar wondered if a Nineties man could have understood him.

"How does it go?" Julie leaned forward. They were not identical twins. Julie's skull was larger than Carol's. The same features on a more expansive skeleton appeared niggardly; Julie's freckles were a crabbed, ungenerous spatter.

"What?"

"The words. What are the words?"

"Not again." Eleanor slapped her own cheek.

"I'm not as smart as you are, Miss Titless No Ass." Carol whinnied. Julie said, "At least I can make the goodies."

"Stop it. Both of you."

"She started it."

"All right." Oscar touched his forehead to the steering wheel. "Priest. I know why bigamy was a crime."

"How does it go?"

"All right. Listen." He inhaled. "You wait until the dom puts meat into your palm."

"I hold my hands cupped like this?" She made a paten of adjacent palms.

"Right. The dom will say, 'Come and feed at my arm. I have given my flesh for you.' Then you say, 'I accept this gift of grace and I am full of thanks.'"

"I accept this gift of grace and I am full of thanks."

"Listen to her."

"Shut up, Eleanor. Say, Guh. Guh. Say the letter 'g' guh. Not huh."

17

"Guhift of guhrace." Eleanor laughed.

"Well . . . All right. Then another dom will bring the cup of blood."

"Just take a sip, dear. Don't drink it all, like you usually do."

"I'm eating for two. Only crows peck."

"Eleanor. Please don't lower yourself."

Eeeeee . . . Oscar thought he had blinked: a nip of shadow taken from the sun's white underbelly. A shell exploded to their left in dense evergreen stands. Shrapnel sprayed: a single shaking of some huge castanet. The forest had caught its force. A billow of small birds went up, but no smoke. In the traffic heads bobbed uncertainly; hands were over temples, defensive salutes. Carol had bruised her cheekbone on the door handle. There was a momentary pressure against the eardrum, a child's blowing there.

"Priest!" Eleanor said. She had been startled. "How did that happen?"

"A misfunction," Oscar shrugged. "And they say weapons production is ten years ahead of consumer goods."

"I accept this gift of grace," said Julie and Carol nervously. "And I am full of thanks."

It was four o'clock. The sun had begun to erect a great lean-to of its shadow, fixing it in a slant down from the crater rim, then eastward. Traffic halted. On the right bank a Model T, its front axle broken, knelt forward, salaamed, a trained camel sitting. A tall fat man kicked the radiator, pulling the kicks, furious, yet wary of thin moccasin soles. His belly eaved over deerskin shorts. There were many corpulent men now. Since the Age of Ecology, food had become both ritual and currency. A man's fat was his social substance. Oscar braked.

"It's Leo." Oscar stood, hips against the wheel. "Leo. Leo. Over here."

"Oscar." Leo's thick glasses were misted with perspiration. He visored them up, waved, then shuffled quickly toward Oscar's car. His mustache sewed together a harelip. Grins showed his ovine upper teeth to the gums. He had learned to smile from the extremities of his mouth. "Priest! Am I glad to see you. Look at that son of a bitch. Got room for Betty and Flora?"

"We'll make room." Horns brayed; a ten-yard gap had opened ahead. "They can sit on Carol and Julie's laps."

"Laps. We haven't got laps," Julie giggled.

"Betty. Flora." Betty's head and shoulders appeared behind the broken car. Leo shouted at the irritable traffic. "Hold your horses, damn it. Flora. Hurry up. You can find a ladies' up at the crater." Flora ran huddled from a paling of cedars; hands masked her groin. "Damn woman. I'm sick of her bladder. Sometimes I think the Ecologists had a good idea. Come on. Come on."

The car moved. Sunlight slanted across the windshield, brushed its tawny film of dust, and made opaqueness. Oscar leaned out to see. Flora sat on Betty's lap; the high stomachs of Carol and Julie bolstered her elbows. Leo wedged down beside Oscar. Eleanor slammed the door. Her nostrils closed; the bridge of her nose furrowed. Leo stank. They could see superstructures of the bridge, half wagon wheels spoked with thick, bolted wooden supports. An elderly man hawked images of Priest at the roadside. Oscar waved him away.

"Thank Priest you came along. We've been stuck here since three o'clock. Walked down to the bridge and back twice, but their damned service phone is out. All I need is to miss signing in." He craned over his right shoulder. "Just look at that ecological disaster. Crack. Like a gun going off. Crack. I hit that big rut back there—"

"The road's in bad shape."

"But the car. The car. I bought it two weeks ago. Priest's bloody arm!" He dropped his fist on the dashboard. "Pardon my language, Eleanor. I've had a trying day. No offense meant, Oscar—but do you Ecotech boys ever get anything right? I installed a new flush system back last month of Paul. Yesterday I sat down." He remembered surprise with his face, eyes lidless. "Broke right in half. Water all over the floor. Right in half. I fell on my wrist—"

"Things must be going well with you, Leo." Oscar smiled. "We still have to use the outhouse."

"Bah—" Leo shrugged. "I was on the waiting list for a year. I keep on top of things, that's all. Never mind, Flora—" He turned around. "You're no lightweight yourself. Just keep your big mouth shut." Leo supported paps with his palms. "Brand-new car. There's got to be a better way."

"It's not easy, Leo. I've just been through this with Eleanor. I get a little tired of complaints. We've got too much data. I wish the Ecologists had burned more books."

"No smoke. Pollution."

"It's one thing to know that bolt A has to be screwed into

hole B—then you have to build a machine that makes bolt A. And the bolt-making machine needs bolts. It's what they used to call Chinese boxes."

"Turn right over there."

"Right?"

"I have a press pass. We can use the service entrance."

They crossed the bridge. Traffic was staggered: the primitive framework would support only two cars. Crater River hushed, blowing, a toothless idiot's mouth sound. The racket of the mortars increased, under them now, not merely above, vibrating sympathies in the wooden roadway's tympanum. The fetuses began to pop up against their husks. The great noise had stimulated them, had already become dark memories. Flora and Betty were allowed to touch. Leo shouted. He closed his right ear with one finger. The guard accepted his pass. A saggy, four-railed gate was levered up, then opened. Oscar drove over the hummocked grazing of a dairy farm. The Model T's inefficient differential made his rear wheels lock and slide. Cows had been herded away from the milk-destroying noise. Two burnished silos butted the sky. A farm dog charged their left running board. It barked. They could not hear, and the dog gagged on excitement, on frustration, bringing up its long tongue again and again.

"Turn here." The road ramped, negotiating oblique ascents of the crater wall. Oscar could see the West Parking Lot above. Leo glanced at Eleanor suddenly. She seemed asleep, arm on the car door, ear on the Y of her armpit. He whispered: Oscar felt his breath. "How do you do it?"

"Read. Read all the time."

"No. Julie and Carol."

"Oh," Oscar laughed. Leo fingered the image of Priest, slid it quickly along the dashboard, a mating chess piece. "Hard work. Positive thought. Patriotism. My country right or wrong."

"I'm a patriot," said Leo seriously. "No one can say I'm not a patriot."

The press area was a gravel peninsula. It had been separated from the West Parking Lot by raw logs, their surface hewn to textures of a ragged, carved turkey breast. The women rushed ahead; for the first time, they had been granted equal privilege at the Feast of Eater. Oscar guessed there were at least two thousand cars in the West Parking Lot. Most had colorful pennants attached to the windshield; it was impossible otherwise to distinguish one car from another. Leo stooped to remove gravel from his moccasin. Oscar stared toward the West Gallery entrance. Over the steep shoulder he saw a colossal profile: the mammoth statue of Priest. Leo clutched his elbow. Eleanor hesitated behind the other women, but when she saw Leo whispering, she strode angrily ahead, through an aisle of cars. Her braid danced from left to right shoulder, back again. A one-legged man hopping.

"Oscar, my friend. Remember when we were in the Volunteer Guards? It's twenty years now."

"Volunteer." Oscar drew a set of earplugs from his pocket. "I always liked that. Volunteer. A drafted volunteer."

22

"Remember big Lois? That Eater holiday down in Southend?"

"Big Lois. Priest! I remember. Do you still see her?" Leo's articulation disturbed him. It was imprecise, blurred, as is speech among the deaf.

"No. Dom's holy name, no. I haven't the time or the inclination. I work a nine-day week. It's not easy running a so-called free press with the Consul's rep looking over your shoulder. I was just being sentimental. Shit, they were good days, weren't they? We shared. You didn't mind my sloppy seconds."

"You had mine, as I recall."

"Ah, well . . . perhaps. I couldn't grow a decent mustache then." Leo put a large red sour ball in his mouth. He sucked. "Would you consider doing me a favor?"

"Yes. What?" Oscar inserted one plug. His left eardrum had burst during the last Feast of Eater. It had bled for days.

"A little nightwork." Leo pulled the fingertips of his left hand, as if removing a glove. "With Betty and Flora. They both like you. You've kept in shape, Oscar. Women go for that craggy, haunted face of yours."

"Swap? Don't you get enough?"

"Oh, no. No. Too much." He raised the backs of both hands against his chest, wriggled fingertips there. "I don't want to touch yours. Priest! That Eleanor scares me half to death." Leo sucked. The red ball edged out through his slit lip, glans through foreskin. "I need children."

"What's that? I didn't hear."

"Don't make fun of me, damn it."

"No. I'm not. I didn't hear." Leo leaned close.

"I said—I need children."

"Oh." Oscar smiled. "Don't worry, they won't put you in the crater for that. Not any more."

"Of course not." Leo touched his armband, then squeezed it: one of three preferred reverences. "But I am embarrassed. I write editorials about the new man, virile, tough, procreative. You know. That sort of thing. Look—even with three wives I bet a change would do you good."

"You're serious?"

"Yes." Leo crunched the candy ball. "Ah—I'm thinking of running for underconsul from Baldwin next year."

"I see."

Leo was puffing. An inverted triangle of sweat, base line across shoulders, apex at buttocks, grew dark on his back. They rested in front of the state souvenir stand. Oscar examined a pair of cheap field glasses. There were icons of Priest with paste rubies set in the arm; postcards; toy mortars that exploded a cork; stereopticon slides taken from the movie *Priest*, which had starred Edric Ekholm; CRATER '81 bumper stickers; a game for five-to-ten-year-olds called Boom!! The entrance to a pleasant prayer glade opened behind the stand: stone benches under weeping willows circled a goldfish pond. A dom exited from the glade. He wore a black rubberized suit, black hood; his left sleeve was scarlet below the biceps. He fingered a rosary of drilled human incisors. The souvenir man wished him a happy Eater. The dom gave him a perfunctory blessing, left fist in left armpit,

24

left elbow up, an amputation. His words did not survive the crater uproar. Leo inclined his head, eyes pressed discreetly shut. Oscar grinned.

"Leo," he said. "Let's talk this thing over. I've got a proposition. Come in here."

A forelock of willow branches screened the bench. Oscar parted it. The granite was chill, powdery with green/white insecticide. Leo unlaced the thonging of his shorts; he hiked them over his belly. Goldfish snouts pocked the water. They ate at a flotsam mash of dying flies and spiders, big mosquitoes. Explosions troubled the pool, inscribed a complex record of their force and distance. Leo sat beside Oscar. He tried to heave right ankle onto left knee. The ankle slipped off, shoved by the fat of his inner thigh. He held it there, one finger hooked in the back of his moccasin. Oscar lit a pipe.

"Well. What do you say, Oscar?"

"Have you read my manuscript?" Leo's ankle fell again. He put a sour ball in his mouth; he crushed it without sucking. "Have you read it?" Leo nodded. "I thought we might arrange a deal: I produce your children. You produce mine."

"Ha." Leo smiled; frowned. "Tell me—honestly, Oscar. Do I look stupid or something?"

"What d'you mean?"

"No. That's what I mean. No. You catch on slowly."

"Why not?"

"Why not? he asks." Leo shook his head. He mouthed two sour balls, tongues in both cheeks. "Why not? It's suicide, that's why. I'd never live to see my children grow

25

up. I'd be running around in there with my hands over my head. And you running right next to me. *The True Book of Priest.* Yes. Yes, indeed. Just what we need. Dom's arm, you've got to be kidding."

"I'm not."

"Then you're insane."

"Come on, Leo. These aren't the old days. Things have loosened up. Anyway, I don't want a best seller. Just some sort of private edition. A few hundred copies."

"My friend, my friend—I'm glad you came to me." Leo put a palm on each of Oscar's shoulders. "I can save you a lot of trouble, a lot of heartache. Just listen to old Leo—for Eleanor's sake, for the sake of your children." He paused; he was panting. "You think I'm a big publisher. No. No, sir—I can't print a menu without permission. And if the state rep isn't watching, at least two men from my Printer's Guild local are on the NIA payroll. This is the sort of thing I can publish." He listed them on his fingers, *"How to Prevent Potato Blight, You and Your Sewage, Venereal Disease: It Can Be Stopped.* Oh, a classic now and then, Shakespeare. Yes, but they couldn't even pass *Julius Caesar.* Dom, Oscar—your book suggests that Priest didn't give his arm for our salvation."

"He didn't. Any asshole knows that," Oscar yelled it. Leo glanced toward the souvenir stand. But the mortars had suppressed Oscar's words. "Look, Leo—the parallels with Christianity are too obvious. He must have found a copy of the New Testament or one of the prayer books. Maybe, who knows, he may have met someone like Xavier Paul.

I'm not sure. No one can be certain. He was a crude, stupid man. Yet he was clever in a way. He understood men."

"Yes. Damn it. Give the devil his due. We wouldn't be here if it wasn't for Priest. I don't care what goes on in there. It's better than suicide."

"What goes on in there stinks. It stinks." Oscar's intensity disconcerted Leo. "There's no need for it. We're not savages any more. And why? It's just to support that sick, power-mad bunch of red arms."

"Keep your voice down."

"You won't print it?"

"No. I won't. I can't. I've no taste for martyrdom."

"Then send it back."

Leo slapped his thighs. "I should have burned the damn thing."

"I have a copy."

"Priest. You are crazy."

"Admit one thing. It's well written, isn't it?"

"I see. Ha!" Leo laughed. He brushed through Oscar's closely cropped hair. He cuffed Oscar's ear. "Vanity? Is that it? Another man of science who wants to be an artist. Yes. Of course it's well written, damn well written. The research on New York in the Ecological Age is fascinating, fabulous. I couldn't put it down. Mind you, I'm not entirely convinced by your characterization of Priest. But, look—write another book if you like. We'll be bringing out some novels in the next few years. Uncontroversial stuff. In fact, the deputy consul's wife has written one."

"Screw you."

27

"Yes." Leo laughed. Then he pushed his tongue through the wet valve of his lip. "Ah, Oscar—you're not planning some sort of scene up in the gallery?"

"No. Not this year. I won't compromise you."

"Good boy. Good boy."

Leo clapped his hands. They stood and stepped sideways through the willow fall. At the souvenir stand Leo bought two Priest amulets, abstract stick figures of silver. A single mortar shell went wild above them: shrieks from a torn throat. The crowd performed calisthenics, knees bent, flat palms at sides of neck. It exploded in the West Parking Lot. Oscar saw the windshield and one fender of a Model T rise through a fifty-foot perpendicular, paddle-wheel over each other, the windshield intact. Next to him an old woman, an honorary Eve of Priest, kissed her armband. Leo turned and began to struggle up the steep dirt path, one yanking hand on a metal banister. Oscar followed him.

"Priest Almighty." Leo gasped. "I think we'd be safer inside the crater. Eco-technology. What a farce."

"It's not bad—I mean statistically. Each mortar shoots at least five hundred rounds a day. Fifteen hundred between Good Monday and Eater."

"Ah—" Leo rested. He stared up at the black/green statue of Priest, now visible against a triple arch of gateway, against the sky. "I don't care what you say. The Feast is a great thing. I remember my first shoot. I was sure I had killed someone. My father gave me a new red bicycle."

"I never try to kill anyone. I try to find an empty sector."

"Look. There are a lot of people up there—they all have a

28

quite different idea of the Feast." Leo started walking. "Just shut up."

"It's barbaric."

"Better to eat than be eaten. Mmmpph-ah. Better than suicide." Leo was cheerful. "Ahhh—I hope you Ecotech people are working on escalators."

"Forty years ago that lip would have been the end of you." Leo stopped. "Better to eat than be eaten."

"That was uncalled for. That was low. You're a scoundrel."

"Better to eat than be eaten. That big ass of yours would have fed a hundred communicants, I bet."

"Ha—" Leo pulled upward. "Better, I suppose, that mankind be eaten to the bone by vultures. If it comes down to me or the common housefly—I'll take me every time, thank you."

"Not so fast. You'll have a heart attack."

"Oscar. Do you really prefer Ecology to human life? Or is it just your latest affectation?"

"There has to be a compromise."

"There is no compromise. History proves it."

"There must be. Look at America."

"Yes. Mmmm. Give a push while you're talking." Oscar placed a palm above each of Leo's kidneys. He heaved: the heavy flesh hurried up along his spine, moving, loose, as though it were transient on him. "America. That was six hundred years ago. It just proves—men can't progress with a too exalted concept of human life. Don't use your nails, damn

29

it." Leo stopped. "By the way. That suggestion I made—about Flora and Betty."

"You retract it."

"Ah . . . well. In your present crazy state I'd rather not be indebted. Thanks anyway."

"Understood. Understood. The point is taken."

They hesitated at the downsloping cobblestone lip of Crater Plaza. Leo mouthed; he inclined his head. Reluctantly Oscar acknowledged its power. The bronze statue of Priest-at-his-feeding was twenty-seven feet tall. It dominated the plaza. Oscar gasped. Abruptly the two hundred mortars had ceased firing. The silence was fierce, a barrier wrenched aside. Oscar almost toppled forward into its great absence. He could hear the rivulet of water that dribbled from Priest's torn half arm. The figure was twisted slightly, at the knee, at the hips, *contrapposto*. There was primitive agony in the expression, yet forbearance and serenity interpenetrated it, occupied the same emotional space-time. This was the finest of A. Bonanno's early works. The face—leathery tissue taut over cheekbone and jaw and prominent brow ridge—approximated the one authentic extant photo of Dominick Priest. The eyes were small and recondite. His occiput extended a perpendicular thrust of neck. Little brain capacity, Oscar thought, little capacity for guilt. Yet he is my father. He is father of us all. Each descended from the first ten women. Those poor fools: his captives; his concubines. The ten Eves of Priest, our second Adam.

Leo knelt on pine-bough cushions. He dipped his right hand and anointed the armband's ruby with water. Oscar's gesture was perfunctory; his fingers did not touch the water. Leo immersed the two amulets he had bought for Betty and Flora. Oscar flipped a ten-dom piece into the fountain. From a loudspeaker the words of Priest, written a hundred years after his death by Dom Alphonsus Connor, echoed over the plaza, "It is said in the Book of Priest, 'Death met me at the garden of jungles. He was hideous: head of deer and snake and bear and fly.'" Leo mouthed the familiar words silently. "'And Death spoke unto me in this wise, "I have freed your people. I have taken life from them." And I, Priest, did answer Death, "Verily man was made to rule over the birds of the sky and the beasts of the field and the fishes of the sea and the insect that burrows under the skin. And I will return man to his inheritance." And Death said unto me, "How will you do this? How? For your people's mouths are stopped and their bowels are shriveled and they have forgotten to make children from their loins. Who will feed them?" And I, Priest, answered Death—"I, the Son, will feed them with my own arm. I will sharpen their teeth and open the passage of their throats. I will make their bowels to enrich the land. I will restore man to his inheritance, so that he may worship my Father. For my Father is not worshiped by deer and bear and snake and fly. My Father is worshiped by man, by the mind and the heart that can compass Him. My Father loves His children. He will make creation to worship Him again."'" Leo nodded. The tape loop repeated, "It is said in the Book of Priest, 'Death met me at the garden . . .'"

They entered the triple gullet of the archway. Each of its keystones was a single incisor; the voussoirs had been shaped to appear dentate. The ramp, though eroded by the scuffing of three hundred years, was a protrusive, bowled tongue. Above the crown: THIS IS TRUTH: ALL THINGS EAT OR ARE EATEN. Beyond, the gravel gallery was thirty yards wide. Spectators milled six deep at the railing. Eastward the gigantic, abstract arrowhead of Crater Cathedral, its point toward the rising sun, funneled the light into a shadowy V. The north and south wings of its transept were flanged; against the wind, they seemed to imply lift. Worshipers who had made their preparatory devotions strolled, chatting, toward it. Oscar and Leo walked left, past a dozen mortar stations. They edged against the gallery wall as two tractors drawing supply trains ground, with short, dynamic jerks, past them. Noses of mortar shells were pyramided there. Leo sensed a lapse in the throng. He lifted his stomach and wedged through. At the rim he drew Oscar, who was shorter, in front of him. His hands settled on Oscar's shoulders. Oscar shook his head. He balanced backward, bracing his heels, bowing his spine. Leo's weight worried him: the iron railing, loose in its upright sockets, seemed to give dangerously above a hundred-foot drop.

Stonehenge was the setting at this Feast of Eater. Oscar thought it apt. Last year's Amazon Jungle panorama had been misconceived. By the third afternoon of dry heat, imported fronds were flabby and brown; the native huts, flimsily constructed thatch, had sagged, seeming tattered whisk brooms from the gallery. Oscar scanned the circular, square-mile floor. Slabs were erect. They were linteled by slabs. Some had been ruined in their design; others had been wrecked by mortar impact. One row of slabs was propped shoulder to shoulder, a loaf of bread fanning. Oscar counted four or five mock Stonehenges: he knew their purpose. Small figures prowled in the mazy stone angles, grouped there by a meretricious promise of shelter. They made convenient targets. Below, fifty yards in, Oscar saw the twenty-foot ditch and the electrified fence, concentric circles within the crater circle, there to prevent victims from assembling near the wall. It was intermission. Blocky orange tractors, bearing the white, red-gouted flag of Priest, crabbed over the crater floor. A dozen hooks furrowed behind on chains; each ripped up a wake of dust, polydactyl clawing hands. Leo offered a sour ball, but Oscar was fasting. He refused.

"Oscar. I've been looking all over for you." It was Eleanor. She pulled him away from the railing. "Come. I want you to watch me shoot."

"All right. Leo—I'll meet you outside the Cathedral entrance."

"Remember. I'm stuck here without you."

"Leo. Betty and Flora are down by the relic stand," Eleanor said. "They've shot already."

"Spending money," Leo said. "Good kill, Eleanor. Congratulations."

"Thank you."

They hurried around the western perimeter. Eleanor trotted: Oscar held the plump braid's tip gently, a rein that canted her chin up as Eleanor picked a way through the crowd. She was excited; she rolled her small breasts upward/ downward with tight fists. The sun had declined; this side of

33

the crater was in shadow. The burly mortars, swabs tonguing upward, seemed another sort of mortar, a chemist's, pestled. Eleanor led him to Station ⚹37; three and seven were her lucky numbers. The stations had an odd designation leftward from the crater entrance. She held reservation tickets 379-37 and 380-37. She handed Oscar the higher number. The ticket adhered to her fingers: Oscar saw on its glossy scarlet patina the whorl of Eleanor's thumbprint and, over it, a circumflex punching of her sharp nail. They waited on line. Two young men described trajectories with their hands; they blew explosions out of bubble cheeks. Saliva froth collected at their mouth corners; it seemed an indication of appetite. Number 375-37 stood just below a spiraled metal staircase that led up/around the mortar platform. Eleanor stapled her arm over Oscar's hips, poking, as she did, the sensitive nub end of his spine.

"I feel horny."

Oscar grunted. Eleanor's times of sexual exultation were rare and tremendous. She saved fantasies toward a tidal release; it occurred often just before her period. Oscar was aroused; and at once, too, he was ashamed. His pleasure would derive from an act of murder.

"Remember now. This is a religious exercise."

"Yes. Yes." She sucked spit back through her long teeth. "I'm going to kill someone."

"Perhaps."

"How many are left out there? How many do you think?"

"A few hundred. It's pretty late in the afternoon."

"I wish—" She closed her eyes. "I wish they weren't all

defectives and criminals. I'd like to kill someone who was really built. Some big, cocky bastard." She leaned close, whispered; she bit his ear lobe. "I'd like you to be out there. Naked."

"Many thanks."

"Just to see what it's like. Not because I don't love you. Because I do." She stood on tiptoe. "I wish I could see better."

"Cruel Eleanor." In a spontaneous convulsion that startled him, she clawed the tight seat of his deerskin pants. Taut material transmitted clawing to his codpiece. "A hundred years ago the killing was done with a club. Man to man. Man to woman. The victim's hands were bound. His ankles were shackled to a stake." Oscar wasn't sure of the details: rituals had differed from principality to principality. He elaborated. He gave her fantasies.

"Priest—that must have been exciting."

"Yes. Better, I think." Oscar frowned. He was disgusted with himself. "People saw what they were doing. They saw the battered skulls. The brains. They understood the meaning of death. In fact that's why the craters were invented. Too many people refused to kill. Also, of course, there weren't enough victims to go around."

"People are getting soft. Soft. Oh!"

The mortars had recommenced. Oscar wobbled the ear plugs in. His head was sealed; instinctively, he opened his mouth to release a cloying pressure. Eleanor had wedged to the rail. Number 375-37 started up the staircase. Gaping, fingers under jaw, Oscar gazed upward. It was a lovely day,

35

but the sky held symptoms of its maturity and decay. Evening winds had materialized: the smoke/dust of explosions registered its direction, slanting up, exploding again, rising to the northeast. Oscar swallowed, swallowed. A bank of approaching cloud lay prone across the western horizon. It threatened the sun; night's closing visor. The throb vibrated in his nose bridge; he breathed nervously and air seemed to escape from his head through the eye corners. His vision jiggled.

Eleanor pumped his arm, pointed. Seventy-five yards beyond the electrified fence, Oscar saw a figure running. Stick legs, stick arms, dot of head at that distance, yet the legs flexed, extended with a high hurdler's windmilling, economical grace. Eleanor shouted; he did not hear. She ate at her fingers. Oscar supposed that the man was in panic. Then the figure slowed, stood still.

He waited with both fists balled overhead. A creeping barrage of mortar bursts strode toward him from the north —one-two, three-four: an iambic walk. He did not move as the wind furled powder debris across his face, obscured him. Then he was visible, nude at the torso, a brown shirt held out on rigid arms, knuckles up. Another shell exploded. The spine arched; the shirt flicked, teasing. Oscar was fascinated. Eleanor had brought the braid around her cheek. She sucked it. Two shells twinned an explosion: with prancing heel steps the figure chased it. He seemed to chide; chin jutted, jerked. A shell hit behind and nearer. Its impact clapped him over the shoulder blades. The figure pirouetted, eager, the shirt

36

easing across his chest. Eleanor pressed her palm against Oscar's belly.

"A matador." She said. "Challenging all of us. Him. I want him. I want to kill him. Do you think I can?" But Oscar could not hear her.

Number 378-37 stepped down. Eleanor raised Oscar's shirt, pinched the fleshy brim of his navel. He wrenched her fingers off. Eleanor laughed and the sound of mortars came from between her teeth. She climbed the stairs; the braid noosed her throat. Oscar didn't think she could kill the matador. He was too near; the trajectory was steep. Oscar watched. The matador waited, inert. He was the only upright figure on the gray/brown plain, and now he had drawn upon himself the whole gallery's attention. Explosions began to clump; they cauliflowered, merging. They approached from three sides, and in the matador's pantomime Oscar could imagine, could personify their massed charge. Not a bull: the remorseless, primitive, hungry, heavy assault of his civilization. Oscar was glad of the image. He was to remember it just before his own death. And, watching then, he was grateful.

The figure toppled. It had not been the mortars. Oscar shoved to the rail. Driving back with his heels, supported on shoulders and neck, the man bridged his body, rib cage uppermost, hands crossed placidly on it. Then he sprawled. The body segmented: legs, abdomen, chest, head, arms. In slow and vicious convulsions the segments strove against each other. Oscar turned away. The shells continued to fall, but now into a void of the man's disinterest. There was something habitual about the spasms; it was physical extravagance by rote. Oscar sensed that he had not been witnessing courage, nor even arrogance, but merely an old madness. He saw Flora and Betty. They walked east along the crater gallery; each held a shako of cotton candy. They ate, jaws sideways, into the pink undermeat, as sharks feed.

A different concussion, the hollow and wet smack of broken fruit. Oscar scanned the concave crater wall. At station ⚹57 or ⚹59, he thought, the mortar barrel had exploded. A torso was draped, face downward, over the platform edge. Large fragments of metal, one spade-shaped, a dorsal fin, were imbedded along the spine. An ambulance moved with cunning haste through the gallery crowd. Eleanor descended the staircase. Oscar had not seen her shoot. She held her palms cupped, fingers interwoven in the standard reverence. The fingers were strangling; their tips were purple, packed with blood.

"He wouldn't let me aim at him. He said it was too close." Oscar did not hear. He recognized her anger, and from wise habit, seemed to ignore it. "Who knows what I hit? Who knows? I'm sick with disappointment. The whole thing was a fraud."

Oscar went up. The platform was circular. Shells had been stacked on a wooden forklift pallet. His gunner stood at the rail; he had been staring at the cracked mortar. The torso had been drawn back. There were two red trails where the wrists had dragged. The rail was curled out; slides of crumbled rock chased down the crater face. Oscar shook his head: the matador was sprinting again. The sun went in. The gunner turned around; his padded helmet was so huge it produced a specious microcephaly. His face seemed childish, unfinished. He took Oscar's identity card, punched it.

"These mortars. Not for shooting so much." He touched the barrel and jerked his hand away. "See. Hot. I don't like this."

Oscar read the lectern chart. The Northeast Crater had been graphed. A green half circle represented impossible angles of elevation. He selected sector YY-99—it was on the northern periphery. Oscar would not see the impact. At the mortar's base, large gears gnashed at each other. His gunner crowbarred with a lever; the mouth inclined, settling in jerks, tooth by tooth. Then it was moved left on a recalcitrant turntable, tumid with heat. YY-99 was locked in. The gunner seemed uncertain, panicky. He lifted a shell from the pallet and carried it, cradling, a newborn child presented to its father. Oscar kissed the blunt nose. He let it nudge the red armband sewn by his mother seventeen years before at the Eater of his majority. The gunner tiptoed on a tripod step stool. He inserted the shell gingerly. Then he wiped the false forehead of his helmet. And Oscar said the ritual words: "I perform this act in the name of Priest and in the name of man, who is, who shall always be, the only master of God's great creation. I kill that I may know life. Go in love without rancor—bring the grace of Priest to those who eat and those who are eaten."

He jerked the lanyard.

THE TRUE BOOK OF PRIEST

LOWING OF WILD COWS awakened him. It was dawn. He had slept on a bunk of broken seats twenty-five rows up. The left field grandstand had collapsed; other prisoners were afraid of the rickety, high superstructure. In strong winds ancient girdering scissored like hinges, moaning; its concrete epidermis crumbled. The spring months had been bitterly cold, but there, above the compound floor, he could be alone. He pulled off the ragged woolen blanket: it preserved smells of horses that had died twenty years before. He lay naked and long. The bowl of his pelvis was deep enough to cup shadows. He stared beyond the center field bleachers. On a wall of the old Bronx Criminal Courts Building underleaves of the universal creeper, dewed and silvery, returned the sun's first signal. A wind blew and the wall seemed to fluctuate, combers of foliage cresting, troughing, as though the building were a dummy of itself painted on canvas flats. It appeared to him that all shapes in the city were provisional: geometry, once its glory, had lost exactitude, had softened. At times the uncertainty of shape and perspective nauseated him.

Cats shouted in the silence of Yankee Prison; its imperfect

crater allowed echoes. Dominick Priest sat up. On a chair back, with a corroded nail he engraved his one hundred tenth mark since the day he had been sentenced: six months' detention for Speaking Aloud, Angered. Across the arena plain, the left field grandstand slumped, upper plate of a jaw that had clamped shut; decorative finial teeth bit unevenly into the outfield earth. Twenty men had been crushed/interred there. For a month as the weather warmed through late May, early June, they had smelled the putrefaction of human flesh, but there was no machinery to lever up the broken girders. Yesterday in a thunderstorm the last great light tower had toppled. Half-gourd lamps lay scattered, windfall fruit, near the bronze memorial plaque:

YANKEE STADIUM

Where, in an age of
brutality and ignorance,
men presumed to compete
against their
brother men.

Priest yawned. Fingertips gathered over his mouth, careful of sounds. Even involuntary noise had been proscribed. He was forty, born more than ten years before the Ecological Decree. He was six feet three inches tall. In formative years his shin and thigh bones had not been warped by the E-diet. Few men were taller than five feet. Few men lived beyond fifty. Below, the stadium floor effervesced with dodging white caps. In all temperate zones natural selection had chosen the dandelion. Only the ubiquitous, botanist-hybrid creeper was a more efficient plant. The dandelion heads were desiccated,

44

sporing. A mutant had evolved; its flowers were five inches across. Puffed by the breeding wind they expanded to white gases. On gusty days any field of mature plants became a death trap. Men had suffocated breathing seeds.

Priest stood, then stretched. He was hungry, but the eating spasms humiliated him; he loathed, too, the enervating symptoms of the E-diet narcotic. He had not eaten in thirty-six hours; by austere habit, he would not feed again for another full day. A crescent sun appeared over the fallen grandstand. He arched his hand against its glare. A phalange of his forefinger was outlined through tissue flesh. Shoals at low tide, his abdominal organs subsided, pulsed, visible in their small business. Dominick Priest's face was Mongoloid; flat planes tautened over large cheekbones, then down/over the jaw. There were suggestions of epicanthi at his eye corners. The brows seemed huge: they were plumped by a prominent skull ridge above the eye. Braided with filth, chestnut hair touched his shoulders, but the beard grew sparsely—a brown hand that cupped his chin, its fingers reaching to lower lip. He sat. His black insect suit was spread to air on the row of seats behind him. He had been bitten often in the night, yet mosquitoes were less prevalent on the stadium's upper deck. A line of septic bites followed his right carotid artery from ear to collarbone. He did not scratch. The first July nights had been humid, the poreless suit had stifled him—though there was no superfluous moisture in his body and he had not perspired for thirty years.

In the lower-deck aisles, in mazed, slanting, ruinous tunnels under the grandstand, Priest's seventy-two fellow prison-

45

ers had begun to wake. Ten or twelve shuffled toward an E-diet fountain set in the lower left ventricle of the stadium's heart shape. The spout bubbled green/gold; it was gemmeous, pretty, unlike the still pastels of meat and fruit. At the third-base dugout a woman lay rigid on her spine. Priest frowned. Over empty dandelion skulls he saw her knees bent up, splayed. She pushed down with both palms as though working shaft of torso loose from pelvis socket. She was in pain. Her head swiveled left/right, eyes vacant, staring apathetically at the ankles of some other prisoner. She had eaten six hours before. The legal E-diet was made from inert substances; it was biodegradable in the human digestive tract. The chemical reaction induced terrific cramps. Human sewage had been outlawed by the Ecological Decree; the E-diet caused only a negligible, odorless trace. Priest's thumb felt the frustrated clench of his stomach. He could remember his own excrement and the liberating stream of urine played high against a tree trunk.

Priest broke a seat. The arm rest bent outward; sprinkles of brown corrosion popped from its metal surface under stress. Priest was angered then. He had commited his crime at the same metabolic time: thirty-six hours without the E-diet tranquilizer. He was not ashamed. Priest cherished anger. It was the analogue of contraction in his hard biceps. Mary, Priest's wife, had caressed both, aroused by her own fear. Anger supplied him with privacy and the status of an eccentric in New Loch. Mary would not look at him when he had eaten the E-diet and his pupils had become furry; when he toyed, nodding, with pebbles or the caked strands

46

of his hair. He ate only at night that his debilitation and the spasms, too like a woman's labor, might be secret. Priest flexed a week-old sprain in his right ankle. It was still swollen, the skin glossy and purple, the skin of an eggplant. He suspected hairline fractures. Stubbornly he forced the joint with both hands. He heard/felt dull crushing, the disintegration of thick, dry soap cakes. When his term ended, Priest would have to walk more than seventy miles.

A tomcat stalked. With exact, patient steps it nudged between the dandelion heads. It had become a carrier: the shuttlecock spores clung in a spume on its fur. Priest saw a female cat, tortoiseshell, one of a few not pregnant. The female lapped at her bosom, chin tucked under. Front left leg/rear right leg, front right leg/rear left leg, the tomcat seemed to strut, all but the nervous tail tip controlled. And Priest remembered the hunting of Mary. He leaned back. He had an erection; he subdued it between his naked thighs. The tomcat leaped; the female eluded him. They churned in gallops across the stadium floor, a wake, a smoky exhaust of burst heads behind them. Priest grinned. As a boy of ten, before the edict against killing all life forms, he had loved to hunt in the woodland, near Bull's Hump. On the Day of Recall Priest had placed his bow and arrow on the wide, open bed of the tractor trailer. His father's rifle lay there, his mother's cutlery and scissors. After that, Priest walked for two weeks alone in the forest, trying his new passivity. On the third day a large gray fox had appeared beside him. Animal and man were both startled: he recalled the fox's tongue out between its teeth. For the first time, Priest was defenseless; he had abdicated as lord of four-footed things. He had run away.

Mary was a nervous doe: slim, small, breastless before her pregnancy, just ten years younger than Priest. Her brown hair was roped back: it twitched. Her sharp nose had nostril cups that seemed to open and shut, to grab at breath. She had willingly been his prey. Their games lasted with the daylight. A kind of courtship; Priest loved its naturalness. Mary understood the terrain around Bull's Hump and Sandeman's Hill. She left a delicate spoor, as women of another age left scents in rooms. After a time they ran nude, clad only with pine resin against the mosquitoes. She had stripped first. No garments were manufactured; those Mary had could not be cleaned. At first Priest was embarrassed. His body was more developed, hirsute, grosser. A secret game, for competition had been forbidden. Mary knew when Priest was angered: in spite, then, he would pretend to lose her vivid trail.

There was scuffing in the concrete tunnel below and to Priest's left. He hid his lap under the blanket. Walters emerged from the tunnel mouth. He walked with the sides of his feet outward, slowly, checking seats in the upper section. He saw Priest. He waved. With one hand Walters rucked up the waistband of his insect-suit pants. He tested footing. Near the tunnel there were yard-wide lapses in the concrete. They were all emaciated; but Walters, Priest knew, was dying: his thinness had a special quality. Under the rib cage a mass of alien flesh squatted, thriving. After common infections, cancer was the most frequent cause of death; E-diet eroded, altered cell walls of stomach and intestine. Tumors

48

had been declared an autonomous life form, no less valid than the life form of their hosts. In any case, the doctors could do little. Drugs, x-rays, surgery were illegal: they destroyed unconscionably high numbers of bacteria.

Priest was irritated. He wanted to be alone. But on several occasions he had spoken to Walters, who was one of the few in Yankee Prison who could still lip-read fluently. Stubborn, with poor verbal aptitude, Priest had never learned the finger language. It still amazed him to watch the others speak, hands intergripped around wrists. Some of the younger prisoners had become so adept that they could talk and listen simultaneously. Priest knew the fingering for "yes" and "no," for a few familiar questions and commands. He knew the basic rules: vowels were indicated by thumb against certain locations on the opposing wristbone, consonants by four fingers against the inner arm. Tightness of grip expressed emotion, interrogatives. Priest remembered a guitarist he had heard before the general prohibition of sound. The finger language was useful in darkness. Artificial light had been proscribed.

Walters sat. Priest guessed that he had eaten during the night. His skin was jaundiced by the E-diet; eye whites were eggnog dashed with pieces of blood. He was panting: commonly in those over forty, the diaphragm became intractable after the spasms. Priest yawned, ignored him. Walters was propped sideways, sitting as nearly all men were compelled to sit, left thigh under right knee joint. The human buttocks had become toncless and empty: an upright sitting posture caused lesions, painful sacroiliac bruises. Walters caught

49

fingertips in his beard. His jaw was dragged open by their weight. Even, glossy rows of white teeth showed, whiter yet contrasted with the yellow lips, oddly youthful, as though he had been carelessly fitted for dentures. No tooth decay had been documented in three decades. Powerful fluorides were added to the E-diet, and there was no food that could legally be chewed.

"Good morning." Walters mouthed the phrase. Though mechanical, his lip articulation was excellent. Once or twice he had interpreted for Priest with the guards.

Priest nodded. He stared out, beyond the high scoreboard, its face now skewed somewhat from the perpendicular—shoulders of a man swimming. On the elevated tracks a train waited precisely where, thirty years before, the city's electrical supply had been cut off. Creeper growth had invaded the windows; it poured out of the train, winged slightly backward to the new sun, suggesting headlong speed. Tiny sucker feet excreted a dilute acid that gradually dissolved stone and metal, even glass. New York City had begun to disintegrate, hard surfaces transmuted into a bitter kind of soil. In New Loch, seventy miles upstate, the indigenous flora had been allowed to reassert itself. But in New York City, even after breakers and seeders had penetrated the pavement, native granite had proved infertile.

"In a good mood again. Uh-huh. I can see that." Priest shrugged. Walters leaned forward, until Priest could conveniently see his lips. "Thinking of your wife? Mary—that's her name, isn't it?" Priest took a flat stone from the pocket of his insect suit. He sucked on it. Without stimulation the saliva glands would atrophy. "God. You sure are a sullen bastard."

"What does that mean?"

"Bastard? Don't you know what bastard means?"

"No. Sulling."

"Sullen?" Walters considered. "You know . . . Real mean. Ugly-tempered. Not too friendly." Priest nodded.

"I am sullen," he said.

Walters, Priest thought, could not speak naturally, not the way Mary spoke. Walters no longer heard the words in his head; there was neither rhythm nor emotion. When Mary spoke, Priest could imagine that he was deaf. Nose, eyes, tongue were engaged; he even saw, thought he saw, vibrations in her pointed Adam's apple.

"Know what I used to do? This time of morning specially." Priest was not interested. "Used to take a big shit, that's what. Right after breakfast. I loved the smell of it. My own shit." Walters palpated the lump under his ribs. "Leastways, I think I did. Maybe after all these years I'm just being sentimental." Priest didn't know the word; he didn't ask its meaning. Walters talked too much. "You ever take a shit, Priest?"

"Until I was ten years."

"Ten. Makes you forty or so. Pretty much what I figured. You keep yourself in good shape. I'm fifty-five myself. Oldest man here, I think. Not in such good shape though." Walters paused. A big mosquito had settled on the right side of his throat. He fanned at it with one cupped hand: the greatest allowable resistance. The mosquito was not deterred. Walters waited until it had finished, then he pulled up the hood of his insect suit, tucked long hair in, around ears. When Walters spoke again his front teeth seemed larger. "I go downstairs in the tunnels where they keep a big pile of dirt. Used to spread it on the field there. Those friggin' cats been doing their business on it. Now me—I never did see no difference between cat shit and man shit. How about you?"

"No." Priest shrugged. "No difference."

"God. My ass hurts. When I was a kid men were big and fat. Beautiful. What I'd like—I'd like to see just one fat man before I die." Priest yawned. "My boring you?" Priest showed indifference with the planing angle of one palm. "I'd like to lip-talk. Down there you take a guy's arm, ask him a simple question—before you know it he's all over you. Least you're no queer, Priest."

Below, through what had been the right-field bull-pen gate, men with green insect suits of the Ecological Guard began entering in ranks. Priest counted twenty—twice the routine shift. He pointed.

Walters followed the trajectory of his finger. "Yeah. I think it's some announcement they're gonna make." Priest queried him, eyebrows lifted. "I don't know, tell the truth. I heard a few rumors. Some big green hat probably had a brainstorm. Maybe its the old virus breathing thing."

"What is that?"

"Bacteria. Viruses. Little animals like bugs that you can't see."

"I know the word." Priest frowned. "What is virus breathing?"

"Oh. Just ordinary breathing." Walters inhaled. "They found when we breathe in, see—well . . . a lot of bacteria in the air get killed. They've known about it for a long time. Doesn't seem like much they can do. Maybe we'll get a different filter for our masks." Priest had lost interest. "You know, I came here with my father. When they used to play baseball. Right down there. This is forty-five years ago, mind you. Now people you talk to, they think those bats in the museum—you know, they think the players used to brain each other with them. It's not true. No, sir. Was kind of a gentle game. But you can't tell people that." Walters held his ribs, watched the hand that held. He was in pain. Priest did not sympathize. He yawned again. "How's the ankle?"

"I can walk." Priest tried to flex the joint. His instep was lozenge-shaped, bloated; the toes appeared vestigial on it.

"I got a big kick out of watching you run. Up and down those steps. I watched you for a whole hour one day. It's been years since I seen someone run like that." Walters grinned; he bent toward Priest. "You don't eat much E-diet, do you? Sometimes your eyes're hardly yellow at all. I mean . . . you better watch out; they'll start getting suspicious."

"That's my business."

"Is it true what they say, Priest? Did you try to kill a guardsman?"

"That's my business."

"I wouldn't put it past you. Ugly, like I say. Course, you'd get more than six months for attempted murder, wouldn't you?" Priest did not answer. Walters supported the tumor with his right hand. The bulge gave reluctantly: under his

53

rubberized suit shirt it seemed a bladder taut with liquids. "How can you stand it without the drug? God—just the bugs 're enough to drive me nuts. Never mind this little friend of mine. I couldn't face things without the drug."

"I want to face things. I'm alive." Priest spat the stone into his hand. "People like you disgust me."

"Have a heart. After all, we both know I'm dying. I'll be dead before your term is up." Walters shook his head. Priest was silent. "Not exactly sympathetic, are you?"

"I didn't ask you to come up here. I have my own problems."

"No. That's true. You're right. We all die alone." Walters sat back. He smoothed the insect suit's pseudo skin with his palm. "Is it the child?" he asked, but Priest hadn't been watching his lips. He waited, repeated. "Is it the child?" Priest did not answer. "You want to see it, don't you? How old would it be now, two months?"

"If it lived. If my wife is alive."

"You were gonna escape. That's my guess. Over the broken roof. That's how you sprained your ankle." Priest stared at him, eyes lidded. The nose root was flat, shiny. Stupid, Walters thought. "Look—I don't care. But it's not smart. Wait. It'll take you three weeks t' get back. They'll stop you at the bridge. Then you'll be stuck in here for another year."

"No. One week. It'll take me one week, six days. I've counted them."

"Not with that ankle. Not without eating." Priest slapped at his own head. The open hand struck across his scalp and forelock. Motes of dust rose into the sunlight. "Okay. Forget I said it. You know best. Let's talk about something else. Did I ever say what I'm in for?" Priest did not acknowledge the question. "Are you watching my lips?"

"Yes. I'm watching your stupid lips. Why are you in here? What could you do?"

"Competition. My third offense. I was playing chess. Some crime. That's what I hate about the rest of them down there. They think they're guilty. They really think they've done something wrong." Walters inhaled. "Worst thing about this life is the boredom. I don't like reading, not that much. Anti-social activity, the judge said. Three-time offender. Degenerate."

"What did you play?"

"Chess."

"I don't know that. How do you play chess?"

"Ah. It's kind of hard to explain right off." Priest accepted Walters' statement; he lost interest. "I made the men out of wood. Dead wood it was; anybody could see that. But the District Officer said I'd cut down a tree. He didn't say it, just sort of hinted. That didn't help my case any. Besides, like I say, it was my third offense."

"Who did you play with?"

"Are you serious?" Walters mimed laughing. "Myself. Who else would play? Signs of social alienation. Signs of unhealthy striving. Inability to accept, the judge said."

"My father played cards. But not after the Day of Recall."

"Yes." Walters leaned closer. "What did your father do? What was his work?"

"He owned a place for cars. Where they could get gasoline." Instinctively the fingers of his hand were shaped, thumb up, middle and forefinger pointing, last fingers curled. Priest held the air as once he had held the triggered gasoline nozzle.

"Tough." Walters pinched his lips. "Dead now?"

"He killed himself." Priest raised one arm. He held it canted at the elbow, forearm parallel to the floor. "He had a machine for lifting cars. He got under it." Deliberately Priest lowered the arm, watched it. "I found him there."

"God—" But he could recognize no concern in Priest's expression. Walters was disturbed. Priest raised the arm, lowered, then dropped it.

"It was after the road breakers came. After my brother died because there was no car to take him where the doctor was."

"Lot of people died like that."

"They said thousands had died in cars. It was better that one man should die because there were no cars."

"Yes. They have all the answers." Walters glanced down. He started. "Priest. Look."

There was a quonset hut near the visitors' bull pen. It had two rooms: left, the wardens' quarters; right, larger, a dormitory where off-duty guardsmen slept. Prisoners were being formed up in two lines, one line at each door. They wore insect suits; some had shrugged on haversacks. The mosquitoes were vicious just after dawn; plastic filter masks had been snapped shut. The first prisoner in each file surrendered his identity card to a guardsman, then entered the hut. Priest turned to Walters: he was nervous. His eyes moved eccentrically; Walters thought they were unrelated in his head. Other guardsmen had begun to fan out over the lower grandstand.

"What is it? What's happening?"

"I don't know," Walters said. "God knows. Let's wait. Let's not go down there just yet."

"They'll come for us. They're looking now. See. See." Priest appraised the broken left-field grandstand.

"You can't escape, Priest, there's too many of them. They've got stun cans. Just wait and see. Relax."

Priest put his insect-suit shirt on; it squeaked over his tacky shoulders. Watching him, Walters thought he could identify Priest, dead, decayed, from his skeleton. The bone structure was unique; flesh did not embellish it. A long, fluted femur rose out of the seat bowl, higher at knee than at pelvis. A shallow mouth of sinew in the flat left buttock opened, closed. He leaned forward. Under the brow shelf, lids had begun to blink, clearing vision excitedly, though there was nothing to see. Priest's ears worked on his scalp. Below, the prisoners waited, feet obediently still, careful of the thick weeds, living things. A cow lowed and, as though out of the sound, wind gusts came. They caught arms in the centrifuge of the stadium walls, forming quick small vortices. Suddenly Priest stood. His hand hit Walters' shoulder.

"Good God," Walters said. A man had emerged from either door of the shack. The two men walked, unopposed, unescorted out along the bull-pen ramp. One waved back.

"Free. Free." Priest said. He almost articulated the word.

"They're letting us free." He began to kick on his insect-suit pants, ignorant of pain at the ankle joint.

"I don't believe it."

"Mary." Priest mouthed.

"I don't believe it." But Priest was nearly to the tunnel and did not see his words.

Pigeons obliterated the sky; for more than an hour now they had flocked. The black, agitating current sprawled half a mile across. Priest could just suppose its tattered eastern fringe, sunlight beyond the Courts Building. The stadium was in rain-forest shadow. The pigeons flew complex and precise formations—six or eight layers that passed freely through each other, shuttling, weft thread under warp thread. The birds were voiceless but transmitted in their wings the sound of sails, at a distance, collapsed by wind. Priest wore white epaulets: fish-scale circles of creamy dung, each yolked with a black dot. His plastic mask was smeared. Glove tips wiped there. Priest had become frenzied with impatience. He was last man in the right-hand column, four positions from the dormitory entrance. The second line had been processed more efficiently. Walters had already left the prison.

Priest chiseled at the wire-mesh nosepiece of his mask. It was crusty with dung; his thwarted outbreathing had begun to fog the plastic. As the faceless guardsmen passed, Priest drew his shoulders back, seemed uncertainly to balance spine on pelvis. His head nodded cleverly, imitated the E-diet stupor. The line moved; now only two men were ahead of him. Priest remembered the terrible running dreams: moon-lit scenery that jerked past him as he trotted over the same square foot of earth, sinking gradually, preparing an upright grave. He had cried out many times: fortunately the guards-men had not traced his sounds. Priest hated the gauzy, dry night gags. Above now, the flocking had begun to dissipate; it ended in three pennanting wakes. The sun reappeared: hot again. Priest unsnapped his insect mask, left it an inch ajar.

A man and a boy waited ahead of him; they were em-braced belly to back. Priest could hear the feeble, shrill fric-tion of their insect-suit skins. From the rear it was a single epicene animal, black, four-footed; two puerile calves stood inside an omega arch of the man's legs. One arm was draped over the boy's right shoulder; it spoke into the curve of his left wrist. Red ants powdered Priest's legs. There was a small rent beneath his left buttock; Priest patched the split with glove fingertips. It was nine o'clock, he guessed. There was just time to reach the Hudson River before nightfall. Near the quonset hut guardsmen loitered, conversing arm to arm. One throttled the E-diet spout off with a long wrench. Ahead, the man's groin mounted the boy's buttocks, sub-sided, mounted, thighs splaying slightly, closing. Priest was aroused; the reaction disgusted him. A guardsman appeared. The boy disengaged himself. His slim shins cuffed the dandelion heads, burst them, moving with gentle agility. He had Mary's physique: wide, small shoulders; last spinal verte-brae curved, tenting out the fleshless buttocks. But his legs were bowed.

59

Mary's legs were hardly bowed. Born eight months before the Decree, she had been breast-fed until the E-diet embittered, ruined her mother's milk. She came from a stone house on State Route 206. Three hundred yards south, the same highway elbowed around Sebastian Priest's filling station and dairy farm. Mary's father had been a dancer/mime, one of the few men who had profited by the Decree. He became celebrated in an age that would not trust entertainment, touring thousands of miles by bicycle until his death six years before from tetanus. Priest had seen him perform once. And, under branch-linked pines, a proscenium arch, Mary re-enacted characters and images that she had stolen from his rehearsals in the oak-beamed study—a satire on the urban life that neither she nor Priest had ever known. In his turn Priest mimed applause. He was confused, disturbed by "The Roaring Subway," "A Night of Television," "Football Players," "The Mayor," "The Cop," "The Rock Group"— more confused, more disturbed by "The Lecher," whose sensual gestures, muted by Mary's nude, straight body, were implicit of things that excited them in a manner they could not understand, that, at last, had made them laugh.

Black crescents faded under Sebastian Priest's fingernails. In those first years of the Decree his cuticles had fattened; calluses and fissures on the knuckles healed; the thumb pad became blue/white, soft, a doll's bolster. He lay full days in his hammock, rocked slightly by winds netted in the tree heads, a book unopened beneath. Leisure without expectation tired Sebastian and Helga Priest. There was neither appetite nor satiety. His mother tidied, dusting the arid toilet bowl, the dishes that had been propped, exhibits from another age, in their tall glass cabinet. Winters were murderous; it was in winter that Dominick Priest had left home. Only twelve families remained near New Loch. Combustion was strictly forbidden except for the spherical bed warmers that produced a closed, continuous chemical reaction and small heat. In five winters the northern population had been decimated. Survivors trekked south toward the new capital, in Tallahassee. Priest's mother and father went to bed during the second week of December, coupled only for metabolic warmth, a two-headed amorphous mass under the covers, five-gallon gasoline cans of E-diet beside them. But their son worked. He constructed a snow house on the slope of Bull's Hump, lined on its floor with rugs and blankets scavenged from the empty town. When he was sixteen, Mary just seven, she had begun to follow him there.

Priest had not known then that she was female. When he knew, it hardly mattered. She appeared soon after the death of his brother. Carlos had been within months of Mary's age; in her, Priest had completed the education of his brother. Mary's unspoiled admiration was pleasant; he could always read her lips easily. They wrestled, they boxed on the sloping blueberry fields, unaware that these games were pre-erotic. Two years later, during the census, they had eluded a squad of six guardsmen ordered into the woods to find them, leaving, as they did in play, a tantalizing, obvious trail around the three-mile circumference of Bull's Hump. Together, arm over arm, prone on Rattler Hill, they had watched the weary and disgruntled squad. In the wide marsh, source of Rope

61

Creek, the guardsmen had been enticed through a treacherous morass. They heard the fat one, Ogilvy, curse aloud, sunk to the hips in a vegetative ooze. Priest had laughed; he loved the hunting games. After a year, however, Mary's spoor had become terse and unimaginative. Then, in a print of her large left toe, Priest discovered blood. He found it again two days later. Priest was puzzled when, bashfully, Mary showed him the wound. Her mother had died; the flow of blood terrified Mary. Priest packed cool mud carefully into her groin. And that winter, when Priest was twenty, Mary eleven, they had first made love.

His prints gashed the snow. They were shapeless; they suggested nothing of the walker but his fury. Mary was not surprised when the snow piston in its cylinder/tunnel did not slide out. She called again just once. Priest sat inside watching his own breath rise, condense, add fractionally to a veneer of ice on the walls. An hour later, when he was certain she had gone, Priest shouldered the door out. Mary stood there: arms, knees turned in on their opposites, a body's instinctive economy. The angle of her nose was made more acute by ice. The snow had melted an inch beneath her heels. Priest had to wrestle Mary's unresponsive body along the four-foot passage, jerking it behind him. He stripped himself; for several moments he jogged wildly. Then he undressed Mary's extremities, vising her feet in his groin, hands in either armpit. But Mary was not so very severely frozen. When her toes began to move they wiggled in an intentful, arousing pulse under his scrotum. Mary had read the illustrated sex manual left on purpose at her house by Ogilvy, the

man she most loathed. Mary educated Priest then: he remembered "The Lecher"; he uncovered the latent instruc-
tions of his biology. And, from their radiant, spendthrift
heat, the snow-house walls shone with melting.

The line had stepped ahead. Priest waited alone outside
the hut door. Guardsmen exited from their dormitory, hauling duffel bags, footlockers. Six men dismantled a temporary
observation tower. The decks of the huge stadium hung
slack-jawed, astonished. Priest was weak with hunger, with a
furious anticipation that wasted the small nourishment in
his body. He needed to release energy: his throat buzzed.
His hand dog-eared the edges of metal shingling on the hut
wall. Lanky, orange garden spiders toiled under the eaves,
chiefly concerned, in a surfeit of prey, with the sanitation of
their webs. A guardsman emerged; he seemed impatient.
Priest could not work the zipper of his identity pocket. It
had rusted; it tore out, chewing the elastic material. Priest
presented his card. The guardsman unsnapped Priest's mask,
corroborated the photograph. With cursory taps he spoke a
short phrase into Priest's wrist. The guardsman walked on,
then glanced back, annoyed. He returned. He shoved Priest
toward the door.

It was dim inside. A single window opened behind the doctor's head. Priest saw red crosses on the green insect-suit
shoulders. A warped plywood board, powdery with the detritus
of termites busy in it, lay across two sawhorses, a makeshift
table. In one corner there were six folding beds, bent in half,
and a high bureau, its empty drawers tongued out. Racks of
equipment lined one wall: manacles, cans of aerosol stun,

63

chemical warmers. The doctor leaned over his table. He was a Negro. His hair expanded upward in a precisely round, air-filled crest. Priest thought of great puffball mushrooms, teeming with spores, that grew where cow pats had fallen. The doctor grasped Priest's arm brusquely, began tapping there.

Priest said, "I can't speak that way." The doctor was reading from a thick dossier and did not see his lips. Priest subdued the grasping hand: made a diagonal slash with his thumbnail, "No."

The doctor glanced up. Priest's interruption irked him. Priest repeated. "I can't speak that way." The doctor released Priest's arm. Priest formed the words exactly. "I can't speak that way. I have never learned." The doctor's lips moved. "I can't see your mouth. Please move to the light."

"Stupid fool." The plywood vibrated under his fist. "Damn it, man—there is no excuse for this. Are you stupid?" Priest backed, edging toward the window's illumination. "Do you understand me?" The doctor's lips were heavily fleshed: to Priest's eyes they pronounced a silent lisp.

"I understand."

"Move your lips slowly. I have not spoken this way in twenty years." Priest mouthed: the doctor shook his head impatiently. "Can you write?"

Priest nodded. The doctor pushed sheets of paper and a broken pencil stub across the plywood. "You have a bad record, Priest." Priest agreed, but he had seen only the last word. "You raised your voice to Thomas Ogilvy. A guardsman. You spoke in anger. You threatened him."

"Yes," he wrote. "He touched me. He raped my wife."

64

"That is no excuse." Priest hesitated, then decided to write nothing. The doctor opened a wooden case on his desk. He removed a black-and-white capsule. He gave the capsule to Priest.

"What is this?" Priest prodded the capsule in his palm. The doctor slapped his arm. "Watch my lips, you great moron. I haven't all day to waste." The doctor licked his lips, as though to improve clarity in his speech. Then he reconsidered. He handed Priest a notice printed on cardboard.

"Yes?"

"Read it. You can read, can't you?" Priest read:

DECREE OF THE COUNCIL IN FULL, PASSED UNANIMOUSLY
July 7, 2035

Whereas it has been ascertained irrefutably by the Council's Emergency Committee on Respiration that the process of breathing has and will continue to destroy and maim innumerable forms of microscopic biological life, we of the Council, convened in full, have decided that man in good conscience can no longer permit this wanton destruction of our fellow creatures, whose right to exist is fully as great as ours. It is therefore decreed that men, in spontaneous free will and contrition, voluntarily accede to the termination of their species.

This decree will be carried out finally not later than July 20, 2035 by all private citizens; not later than Aug. 1, 2035 by all officers of the Council.

It is hoped, brethren, that you will donate your physical bodies to the earth in such a manner that the heinous crimes of murder and pollution committed by our race throughout history may in some small way find redress.

Go now in peace and love.

"I don't understand."

"What?" The doctor had not seen Priest's mouth. He was fitting small articles into a torn canvas bag.

"I don't understand this."

"No? But it's very simple, my stupid friend." The doctor smiled. "You have seven days. This is July 13. Can you understand what I'm saying?" Priest nodded. "The pill I gave you. It brings death in thirty seconds. Painless. No pain. Do you understand?" But Priest had written on the paper, "What have I done?"

"Oh, God. Stupid. Stupid." Exasperated, the doctor began combing fingers through his dense, grizzled beard. "Didn't you read it? Didn't you read the paper?" Priest nodded. "It's all we've done. All men. For thousands of years. Who do we think we are—God Almighty? How can we dare to take life? All life is sacred. We can't keep committing murder. Do you understand, all life is sacred?" Priest blinked. He wrote quickly, "I am alive."

The doctor read. He frowned. "So. That's the way it is. Yes. Just as I thought—a radical." Priest checked the moving lips warily. "I give you fair warning, Priest. If I make a sign, six men will come in here. I can have your pill administered now. I'm tempted to do it." The doctor made an exaggerative swallow. "Do you want that?"

"No." Priest raised his palm. "No."

"Priest, listen to me. I know what you're thinking. I can see it in those vicious pig's eyes of yours. Forget it. You can't escape. The full Guard will be left alive as long as it takes. They'll hunt down anyone whose card hasn't been

66

collected. The thing, you see, has been planned very carefully." Priest had not paid attention to the doctor's lips. He stared at the pill. "You understand now?"

Priest nodded.

"Then keep your eyes on my mouth, damn it." The doctor extracted a duplicate form. He copied data onto it from Priest's identity card. "Where will you end?" Priest frowned. The doctor isolated each word. "Where will you die?" Priest wrote, "With my family."

The doctor consulted Priest's identity card. "New Loch, New York?"

"Yes."

"Is that across the river?" Priest hesitated. "Across the river? The Hudson?"

"Yes."

"You can't go there." Priest lunged forward. The sheet of plywood butted the doctor's stomach. His move was startling, fierce. The doctor grasped a chemical warmer, then backed sideways.

"I'm going home to see my wife. I have a child—"

"Shut up, you big dumb ox. I can't understand that gibberish anyway," the doctor snarled. "Another move like that and you leave here a dead man." Priest apologized with his hands. "I said. You can't go there. The bridge is down. The George Washington Bridge."

Priest mouthed, "The bridge."

"You can't swim the Hudson, Priest. No one knows what's going on over there in Jersey—we've been cut off for two weeks. You'd better make plans to die here." The doctor returned Priest's identity card. "You have only seven days anyway—not time enough to walk, even if you could cross the Hudson. We were perhaps a little slow getting this decree around to the prisons. Many private citizens have died by now. Members of your family have no doubt already taken final steps." He bent over the form. His face became shadowed; it was silent to Priest's eyes. Priest repeated, "The bridge. The bridge. The bridge is down." The doctor watched him. "Some of our prisoners have shown interest in fertilizing the New York City parks. Several areas of Central Park, for instance, are still badly undergrown. I can issue permission for you to cross the Harlem River at 149th Street. You'll have plenty of time to reach Manhattan Central by the twentieth of July." Priest tongued his lips. "Are you listening?"

"Yes."

"Will you want to fertilize the park?"

Priest nodded. The doctor wrote; then he tore off the original. Priest folded it four times, crammed it into his identity pocket. "You can cross the Harlem River at 149th Street. I've written permission on the form. You will be expected at Central Park before the twentieth. Contact Guards Major Adam Tarboosh at Tavern Headquarters. He will provide grave space and interment." The doctor closed his bag. "Make sure you show up there. If you don't, Guards Major Tarboosh will have an alarm out for you in twenty minutes and—wake up man. I'm talking to you."

"Yes. I thank you."

"Take my advice. Drink some E-diet before you go. Your

skin is too white. We'll be shutting down the public fountains in a few days. You can go." He gestured toward the hut door.

"My ankle," Priest said. The doctor did not understand. Priest wrote, "I sprained my ankle. I need support to walk."

The doctor considered; then he opened a footlocker under the table. He gave Priest a frayed, dirty elastic bandage. Priest made the sign of thanks. He jammed the bandage into his thigh pouch. The doctor escorted him out. "Make your peace, Priest." In sunlight the doctor's words seemed amplified. "You don't understand. You can't expect to: you have no education. You don't know our history. But this will be for the best. The Council is right. Man has brought nothing but destruction and misery to the earth. Destruction and misery and filth and war. Make your peace."

"I will," Priest said.

Walters had waited for him under the el. The creeper amazed Priest: a low vegetative swell came south, urged by the wind, along a quarter-mile section of River Avenue. It rose over hidden sandbars of curbstone, of abandoned cars; it broke silently around Priest's shins, then traveled beyond. The creeper's choppy surface climbed building façades, sank trees whose naked mast tips only poked through. The perspective was vertiginous, sickening. Where sunlight had not opened them, yellow creeper buds were crinkly tight sphincters. A dry candle smell exuded: pollen thick as dust beaten from pillows. The dense bed of creeper growth and creeper humus gave under him; it surprised his bad ankle. Priest approached the el. In an orbiting ball, bumblebees disengaged themselves near his feet. Priest lifted one arm, apprehensive. He was afraid of bees. Walters grinned: big teeth. Priest walked toward him. He moved in a strut, as though crossing deep snow. There were many bees near Walters' face, seeming attracted there. Walters did not show concern; his mask was open.

"It's been coming to this," Walters mouthed. "I'm glad. I'm glad." He yanked a creeper vine with his left hand. Bees were shaken out. Priest stepped away. One hovered near Walters' eye: blur of wing fanned blur of lash. Walters did not blink.

Priest unsnapped the mask so that Walters could read his lips. "The bridge is down."

"Which? The big one—over the Hudson?" Priest nodded, frowned. "You can't swim that, Priest. You haven't got time anyway. They were real slow telling us."

"I will get across."

"How? The tunnels are blocked. A raft? Currents would drag you down to the ocean."

"I will get across." Walters shrugged.

"I'm going to enjoy killing this." He pulled up his insect-suit shirt. Abdominal muscles had learned to flex the tumor. It moved. "Thought you could live without me, didn't you?"

"I have to go." The bees worried him. Priest closed his mask.

"Go." Walters waved a hand cheerfully. "Good luck. You're crazy, God knows. But good luck."

Priest stepped forward. He grasped Walters' arm and

pressed fore, middle, ring fingers together: a tight triangle. It meant good-by, one of the few signs he knew. Walters nodded. "It's been coming to this. Dead by our own free will. Thank God—we didn't deserve to live."

Perhaps Priest answered him; Walters could not see. The bulging wire-mesh eyes and nose in the plastic mask seemed stupid. It was the smooth, simple face of an insect.

SEVERAL HUNDRED COWS milled near the riverbank. They were uneasy; their lowing was querulous. Priest crossed the still floe of concrete rubble, girders. A gargantuan road crusher lay upended, its cab flat; one half-track was broken, treads scattered, bits of an unstrung necklace. Thirty years before, the crusher's weight and the battery of its twenty-four jackhammers had collapsed the Major Deegan Expressway. Priest scooped into the rear hopper. Aged green creeper seeds were stored there yet, large as walnuts, lima-bean shaped, several half sprouted from the nourishment in their fat cotyledons. Priest tossed a handful toward the railroad tracks, toward the Harlem River. Priest wondered if he could swim across.

The Macombs Dam Drawbridge had been open for three decades. Its middle span was swiveled out at a 60-degree angle. A goatee of creeper vines reached from roadway to river, carded below by the sluggish current. Upper levels of the old girderwork supported a rookery metropolis. Ravens strode fussily backward/forward through the steel fenestration, balancing with dark wing bursts. Priest saw thick, shredded bundles: nests. He judged it was possible. Here, though he was a poor swimmer, Priest could halve the distance. An artificial island housed the bridge's central pivot; the island seemed a barge, prowed, with wooden bulkheads. Eight-foot cattails grew on it. Priest planned to rest there.

His ankle ached. Priest stepped across four double lines of track. In one place the rails had been tormented: made molten, crowbarred up/back on themselves, knotted. Ties were charred. Priest knew of railroads. The Erie-Lackawanna had run just west of New Loch. He had seen a diesel locomotive once: he had been small then; the recollection was exaggerated, massive. Priest appreciated power. He stooped to touch the third rail. He paused. South, across the Harlem River, Priest observed a square cloud, mesalike, sheared flat by high air currents. The fire, he estimated, was in Manhattan Central. After three weeks of drought, the creeper undergrowth was brittle, eager kindling. But he anticipated no danger: the cloud was three miles south; winds were against it.

But the cows did worry Priest. They had crowded into a short peninsula: this extended to a pier where once freight cars had been loaded onto river barges. There was sparse grazing on the peninsula. Cows could not eat creeper leaves. The herd's bulk, perhaps four hundred individuals, was south, near the railroad pier, but a half dozen rows separated Priest from the river. Irritated by hunger, the cows wandered in an aimless pattern. Five or six bulls rammed through the pack, initiating busy, short-lived ripples of sexual panic. Priest trampled gritty burdock and Canada thistle,

73

some hybrid plants ten feet high. Beyond this, where weeds had been cropped low, he approached the shifting, anxious periphery of the herd.

Priest understood cows. His mother had managed a modest dairy farm. Priest remembered the night she had unpenned her cows, two days after the Decree, shooing the herd out through an open gate, her own voice bovine and sonorous. In those days Helga Priest had been a burly woman, chestnut braids spiraled on her head, the bit of a wide, dull drill. For Priest the child, that first Decree year had been fantastic: his mother's ample body had wasted with the summer. Her hefty bosom appeared at first to tauten, as if erecting itself, rising; then the breasts vanished, D cups of the brassiere, which she wore from habit, became deflated, crushed beneath her sweater. When she hugged him, there were no consoling surfaces: she seemed suddenly virile. But that second day of the Decree, when she led her cows away, Helga Priest seemed to roll in walking, as men will move heavy, square objects, corner to corner to corner. Until the udders dried she went out secretly before dawn to milk them, spraying the earth. That second night, after she had returned, Priest watched his mother clean manure from the milking pens. He was afraid of her sadness. She shoveled and brushed with stolid industry. Then she bent, plunged one hand to the wrist in manure. She squatted for several minutes. Priest knew her fingers were flexing.

The cows overlapped, six tiers of tight brickwork, between Priest and the bollard-lined riverbank. He slid under the first cow's chest, not behind her, wary of the hoofs.

74

They were starved, udders small as gloves. Half wore tough, yellowish beards of slaver flecked with blood. There was an odor of disease. Priest penetrated slowly deeper into the herd. His progress was careful, painstaking, without abrupt starts. The animals were restless around him. Grass grew in niggardly, separate tufts. Priest heard water purling against the jetty side; then he stood on the five-foot-wide lip of concrete. Thirty yards to the right, masked by a thicket of weeds, he saw where the concrete lip ended above a shallow, rocky cove. He could swim from there.

Priest heard a new tone in the lowing: it was more shrill, staccato. Priest turned; he tiptoed, stared back. After several moments he could distinguish barking: a pack of wild dogs. Then, near the railroad, portions of the herd began to run. They were crazed. They doubled back across the peninsula, toward him, toward the river, as if to make the intersection of a figure eight. Lead cows were loping; they stumbled, unable to reach a gallop. On the left flank Priest saw pairs of clever, murderous poodles. They savaged the kicking hamstrings. Priest edged hurriedly toward the cove. But cows on the jetty pavement had become apprehensive of the dogs, of the charging herd. They milled dangerously; their flanks jolted him. Priest watched the leaders close, perhaps a dozen head across. Quickly he embraced a bollard neck and swung around on it, outward, toes digging for purchase in the concrete bank. He hung over the water.

As the vanguard struck it, a line of cows at the riverbank seemed to bulge outward through thirty yards. Some reared on hind quarters, wedged up by crowding. Then they began toppling into the river. A few did not resist: they plunged forward in gangly leaps. Most huddled on their knees until by inches they were nudged over. Priest clutched the bollard. He heard the hissing friction of hide against its corroded metal. A cow went over near him, hoofs upward; Priest was drenched by the splash. His fingers were pinned against the bollard: one cow had anchored its side desperately against the metal. Its large head craned around to him, forehoofs precariously on the brim of concrete. Priest chewed his lower lip; even through gloves his knuckles were bruised. The cow lowed and Priest saw profoundly along its white, furred tongue. Then it was butted in the haunches. The cow inclined forward, and concrete edges chipped off neatly under its front hoofs. He recognized terror in its eyes. It fell, jostling him. To his left, cows from the panicked vanguard ran willingly into the river. Then the whole herd was urged outward/sideways. A dozen cows fell simultaneously. The compounded impact was thunderous. When they struck flank first, a thin spray was slapped from the river's surface.

The panic subsided. Abruptly the cows discovered grass and ate. Downstream, Priest saw a shoal of humped backs, cows treading water awkwardly toward exhaustion and death. He did not feel concern; Priest was tired of animals. He pulled himself onto the jetty. There were coarse brown hairs between the glove fingers of his left hand. He walked upriver along the pavement. The small cove was stagnant. Brush carried down by the current had woven a breakwater around the rocks that lined its mouth. Green algae wallowed in plump tufts. Priest watched, amazed. He saw a ten-yard-square mesh of water striders, thick as hair. Mosquitoes rose out of the burdock and Canada thistle surrounding the cove. Priest sat on the jetty's end. His legs dangled over the seething hair mass, and the shadow cast by his feet appeared substantial. The striders shied away from it; they clambered on top of each other, heaping five or six layers deep. Priest was disgusted, fascinated. He played there for a moment. Then he heard the near barking of dogs. The pack, he guessed, was now just above him, screened by the weeds.

Priest stripped off his insect suit quickly. At once mosquitoes swarmed on his back: it became hirsute with them, across shoulder blades, over kidneys. A poodle appeared between weed stalks above the inlet. It was disconcerted to see him there: it backed. Calmly, shoulders hunched, Priest tied off his pants legs, then crammed a boot into each elastic knee. He stuffed his shirt into the waist, careful to pad the plastic insect mask so that it would not crack. The poodle reappeared; Priest counted perhaps eight other dogs with it now, chiefly the smaller breeds: spaniels and terriers. They growled as if at a signal, heads low between shoulders, jaws protrusive. Priest smiled. He spat at them, but his mouth had no moisture. The dogs began to flank him: pack strategy evolved during the thirty years of their dominance in the city. Some disappeared left into weeds; some worked right to interdict the jetty edge. They growled encouragement to each other. Priest strapped the belt around his waist. Mosquitoes feeding on his prepuce had caused an erection. The stuffed pants dangled at his hip from a single belt loop. Several dogs were near the concrete edge. Priest bent, scooped putrid water, and dashed it at them. One yelped; Priest grinned. He stepped into the teeming growth of striders. Algae broke apart and gas bubbles carried up a stinking winy odor. The water was only a foot deep. The growling ended. The dogs began to back, surprised—they had not seen a man swim before. Barefoot, Priest cautiously negotiated the rockbound breakwater. Then he knelt and pushed off into the river, mosquitoes lifting from his back as the water rose.

Riotous fish glanced against his thighs and chest. The river was alive. Priest became fatigued after the first twenty strokes. His insect suit was too buoyant; it lurched into the even rhythm of his legs. He kept his face up. Swallowing water had been prohibited: Priest thought he was being watched by guardsmen on the Manhattan shore. A cage of branches floated past him: there were squirrels in it. Priest did not look ahead, afraid the prospect would dishearten him. The ankle was sore: it hurt when kept rigid; slack, the kicking buffeted sinews painfully. He counted one-two, one-two, as arms hugged water in against his chest. Priest's open, smooth strokes became circumscribed and clumsy. He began to stroke only at the elbows. He was panting. He spewed water out, guzzled some involuntarily. Priest swam for ten minutes, his own coxswain, calling one-two, one-two—then, as he tired, Ma-ry, Ma-ry, Ma-ry. He looked up.

He had made an error. Unaware, he had permitted currents to draw him down, almost beyond the island's prow.

Priest thrashed around, upstream. The joint of his ankle seemed to desocket. For a moment he merely treaded water, head up, maintaining his way against the current. Carried past the island, he would certainly drown; he could not swim the river's full width. The bundle of his insect suit rose, a treacherous, unbalancing rudder: in despair he nearly cast it free. His arm muscles had cramped; they were hard, osseous: he could not raise arms above the level of his shoulders. The slimed, wooden bulkheads were just thirty feet ahead of him. Furiously Priest began to dog-paddle, stroking even at the finger joints. He frog-kicked, and very slowly his lower body came to the surface. Bobbing, the soft, half-inflated insect suit probed between his legs, and it seemed then the sensuous and gentle touch of death. Priest became deliberate: he watched the tip of his nose: eyes crossed on it. His gasping became hoarse. He achieved a choppy, wasteful rhythm. Priest moved through pain to insensibility. His nose tip was a long snowbank: he allowed it to blind and numb him. When Priest reached the island he was startled. His forehead crashed against the wood.

He flailed out for a hold, not able to stretch higher than four inches above his head. His vision was blurred; blinking would not clear river water from it. E-diet had stunted the natural lubrication of his eyes. Priest could find no useful lapse in the island's slick bulkhead. He began to drift again. Reluctantly he stroked upstream, swimming with the joints of his wrists, legs in paralysis. Twenty feet beyond, he touched an inch-wide knothole. There he hung the full weight of his body on fore and middle fingers. He tried to straighten: his knees and arms were locked in the exigencies of his long dog-paddle. Left calf began cramping; he could not quite reach down to massage it. The pain boosted at his foot arch like a sharp metal jodhpur strap. He unbuckled the belt; on a third attempt he managed to lob his insect suit over the five-foot-high rampart. He alternated arms, inserted fore and middle fingers of his left hand into the knothole. He dangled there. The water was warm and it flumed pleasantly under his spine. There was a susurrant rustle where it combed through a torrent of creeper vines that poured off the drawbridge brink. Fish pocked the surface around him: as if the river had just come to a boil.

He could not wait. It was probably three o'clock: Priest hoped to reach the Hudson before nightfall. He had to scale the wall. His insect-suit equipment was on the island; he needed an hour's genuine rest. He began to thrust upstream, paddling at times, scraping along the wall with the slight friction of his toe- and fingernails. A seagull landed on the ledge above him. He discovered a larger knothole; he rested, his entire hand grasped in its D shape. Then he pushed off. He hesitated, paddled back. Priest had felt small uncertainties in the wood. He reinserted his right hand and, with left palm braced against the bulwark, he wrenched outward. The wood shivered. Priest pulled again. He heard creaking. Head against the boards, he waited until his strength returned. He changed hands, but the left was weaker. After a moment he let his knees float up, then with half a somersault, he brought his bare feet against the wall, straddling the suspect board. He pulled, eyes closed. It moved outward as a door would, two inches ajar. He wedged into the crack, levering with hands, butting with temple. The plank split on a line the shape of a lightning bolt, held in place only by thin wood slivers. Priest wrestled it away from the bulwark. It floated downstream. Behind, he saw a labyrinthine, frenzied hive of ants. The sunlight had stunned them; thousands of gray-white eggs, pontoon-shaped, dropped into the river. The wood underskeleton of the island was rotted. Horizontal boards had been placed at foot-wide intervals. It was a ladder.

The ants swarmed: their eggs vanished, drained down into the artificial island's heart. Priest inhaled. His ears imprisoned a rushing sound; they were skinned over by membranes of water. He fingered a rung eighteen inches above his head, breaking off loose wood fragments. He tried his weight on it. The board held. Priest thrashed out with his feet and heaved the other arm alongside. He chinned up, running clumsily to the water's surface. His soles captured a rung. Pointed splinters wedged under his big toenail. He was out of the water; gravity shoved down, his spine curved. Priest's own reconstituted weight winded him. Carefully he worked upward in the narrow chimney, then his stomach folded over the island edge, forehead pushed between the tight pulpy cattail roots. Priest gasped. Clutching fasces of stalks, he pulled upright. He barged ahead, leaned into the cattails, letting their spongy resilience support him. He wanted a clearing to lie down in. The cattails seemed to thin several feet beyond him. He staggered forward. He fell headlong into the pool.

It was threaded with life. Priest's fear drove him, thrashing, above the surface. His right fist came out. It was clutched by gray, inch-thick eels: terrible new fingers on it. Priest went under. Horror took co-ordination from his arms and legs. A terrific, tarry stench rose. He could not swim in the roped mass. Eels were dying of their own population. The water was tinted black/purple with excrement. Panicked, too, the eels clung to his lower body. He was concerned for his privates. His fingers grabbed there. He sank again; Priest shouted. And the seagull, hearing a human voice for the first time, flapped up, toward the ocean.

The 155th Street viaduct had collapsed halfway. Priest examined the terrain. Three blocks left, under Coogan's Bluff, the viaduct began again, a precipitous, hundred-foot-high cliff at that point. On either side of it there were insubstantial square spiral staircases. He saw no other means of ascending the bluff, then of crossing four long blocks west to the Hudson. It was serene on the Harlem River shore. Priest guessed that the viaduct had fallen recently. Creeper growth had not yet met across the jumbled moraine of concrete and asphalt and girdering. An ancient glue factory stood opposite. There were limp, frayed Guard flags—the globe on a field of green—above it. Priest had seen no guardsmen. Across the viaduct a cluster of development apartments, their four wings forming crosses, were trousered with the creeper to half a thirty-story height. South, smoke from the fire drifted, attenuating, over the Triboro Bridge. It had not traveled nearer.

Priest drew his insect suit on. He was nauseated. In his swim from the island, he had swallowed water. The absorbency of stomach linings had atrophied: water lay in an active blister beneath the skin of his abdomen. It shifted when he moved; Priest remembered the carpenter's level in his father's toolbox. He leaned over the concrete riverbank. The bubble of water under him threatened to rupture. It was painful: a pain that involved his spine's full length. He picked up a stick and worked it into his throat, played there coyly, exciting dormant reflexes. Water came up. Priest turned onto his back. It was six o'clock. The sky had cleared: diagonals of sunlight crossed below it, but the blue dome was not refreshed; it darkened.

A good breeze had begun to blow toward the river; mosquitoes could not judge their approach. But the bees were ballasted, and there was a species of heavy, black-green fly that had evolved with the creeper; the flies hung in grape bunches, adhering to each other on the underside of leaves. Their detritus and eggs were indistinguishable: white, glutinous. For breeding they preferred the human scalp. Priest hated insect sounds. He understood their stinging; he appreciated its necessity. But the sounds perturbed him. The strident warble of mosquitoes, varying only with distance; the bees' monitory drone; liquid sputterings of the blue-green fly. He did not understand that: he associated it with madness and death. In her final days, an unvaried humming had come from his mother's body, not precisely audible, but there at his fingertips when he touched her forehead.

Priest cowled his head, tucking ends of hair in. The musk of eels permeated his insect suit; his chest, in the suit, had their texture. He mouthed the word, eel: the word, too, was teleost and sinuous. Priest remembered the shout. He punched his face once under the cheekbone, ashamed of weakness. The island had been hollow, rectangle within rectangle, but the pool, though profound at its center, had a shallow, stepped end. Once over his fear, Priest had been able to walk out. The eels had sucker mouths in a column, ocarina stops, under the tail. His thighs and loins had become shaggy with them. Out of water, however, the sucker mouths lost vacuum. The eels dropped off. Priest swathed his right ankle with the elastic bandage: alternately around instep, around heel. He worked into the shin-high rubber boot, then flexed his ankle. The bandage was restrictive: his small toes were starved of blood. He unwrapped the ankle, distributing elastic more evenly over foot, around lower leg. Priest stood.

He walked parallel to the viaduct's debris. Some stanchions had remained upright, holding crow's nests of the old roadway. Priest hurried. He sucked his stone. The river water had made him hungry. The left staircase, on the south, appeared corroded halfway up: broken steel was braced by the creeper growth. Priest stared across the rubble. A car had fallen; it stood upended, fenders elbows, some human figure hand-standing. The northern staircase seemed sound. Something fell from the brink of the viaduct. It was solid, perhaps a stone. Curt, muffled echoes rang beneath the remaining length of the structure. Priest thought he saw a face peering down. He backed under the first whole arch. Above, many bats hung, teats of a bitch, from the riveted metal supports. Priest smiled, then touched his cheek. He was afraid of heights.

Priest gazed downtown along Eighth Avenue. He could see three miles into the city, to the smoke wall. At its base the smoke was more active, darker, producing there a braid of perfect billows. He could not see flame. Priest's vision was good; he had never developed the red/green color blindness endemic since the E-diet. Creeper had drifted in corners of Eighth Avenue. Building walls appeared to slouch near the street. A pack of animals loped uptown, now perhaps ten, perhaps five blocks away. Priest could not be certain if they were cows or wild pigs or dogs: the perspective was deceiving, without reference. Priest turned, then stepped up onto the viaduct wreckage. He began crossing toward the northern staircase.

Priest hesitated. A storefront door was pushed out on 155th Street, opposite the viaduct. It had been a barber-shop once, in an era when hair and beard trimming were permitted. The reds/whites of its pole were stark in contrast with the omnipresent dark green; for some chemical reason the creeper had not rooted on it. A display window had been neatly etched by the vine's acids; S strips had fallen out. The guardsman shoved through. He was a gnome. His legs had been bowed severely; they walked in arcs, straddling, as though set to shinny up trees. Priest ducked, then sidled toward the Viaduct, but he had waited too long. The guardsman signaled peremptorily. With reluctance Priest hobbled toward the barbershop, one forefinger slitting along his identity pocket. On the guardsman's left cheek, blue-green flies adhered, making a second sideburn. His mask was unsnapped; his hood lay rolled behind his neck. He did not brush the flies off. Priest noted that his pupils were swollen, furred. The guardsman moved deliberately, watching each hand, each finger on each hand, while it functioned. He examined Priest's card with stupid concentration. There was caked blood on his beard. Unconsciously, anaesthetized to pain, he had been devouring his lower lip: one corner was gone and a worm flap of skin protruded. Stun cans hung outward in their holsters. Priest presented the doctor's safe-conduct. He was worried: the writing had been blurred by river water; the guardsman, however, thought this a trick of his own unfocused vision. He nodded, nodded. He touched Priest's forearm and spelled a short phrase, repeated it. The guardsman laughed; his breath was sugary. He handed back Priest's papers.

The guardsman tottered backward on his heels, elbows rowing for balance. Then he swiveled. He was crouched by the grotesque warp of his legs, as men begin to lift a heavy object. He stumbled toward Eighth Avenue. Priest wadded the papers into his pocket. Guardsmen, he knew, had easy access to the E-diet narcotic. Hands on knees, the guardsman stopped. Then he settled forward ungracefully, buttocks up, into the creeper bed. He sucked his thumb there; perhaps he ate it. Priest heard barking. The pack of animals was now only one block away; they were not cows or wild pigs. Priest hurried over the debris. Creeper had choked the metal staircase skeleton. Priest remembered the roots that would jam ceramic drainage pipes on Sebastian Priest's farm. He parted a drape of vines at the entrance; he used his pelvis as a lever, drew hinge sounds from the thick, horny vines. Ahead, squirrels scampered agilely up; they stopped to grind their teeth. The twisting staircase was a nest. Priest walked prone, on his back, on his stomach, swinging through the mesh trapeze. His progress was easier when the staircase had doubled once back on itself, but the landing floor had fallen out and Priest was forced to bridge it on a latticework of fragile vines. His left leg snapped through to the knee; he hung from his armpits over the street. Priest's breath exploded the snaps of his mask open. His eyes could not countenance the long drop; they flickered up/under his lids.

Mary was fourteen when she discovered a monocular cave on the cliff face, nearly two hundred feet above the ground. As some complex sinus might, a rock chimney wound from the forehead of Bull's Hump, downward to this single eye. Rudimentary steps had been chiseled into its sides. At bottom of the sinusway, a slate ledge lipped the cliff, thirty yards to the cave mouth. The ledge was fractured, powdery: each crossing diminished it. At best it had been six inches wide. Inside the cave, under a decade's accumulation of dust, they found a skeleton, two rotted mattresses, empty food cans, some pre-Era coins, and a Bible that had been the bassinet of young rodents. An area from Bull's Hump to the Hudson was a stronghold of Christian Nihilist fanatics just after the Decree. Mary and Priest, on easy terms with death, had tossed the skeleton, bone by bone, into pine boughs below. Though the ledge passage had horrified Priest, Mary and he lived there throughout the summer. Mary had no fear; Priest was ashamed of his terror. She sensed it: whenever they had ascended the chimney, Priest, in a terrific reflex, became foolish and reckless. Once he had captured a rattlesnake with his bare hands, shaping it into a scarf, a belt, a jump rope. Mary was afraid of snakes, and Priest had satirized her fear.

Their last visit had been in November, after an early, wet snow. Mary went first: she used handholds perfunctorily. The concavities of her naked body complemented elbows and dimples in the cliff façade. But Priest's weight had loosened shale. The ledge dropped out behind, delayed reactions that scurried after his feet, a deadly, hot fuse. Fear made him nimble. He hurled his body to the wider cave apron. There Priest shammed an ankle sprain, the same ankle, he remembered, that now troubled him on the viaduct staircase. Only a few honed shale blades remained of the ledge. Mary, who weighed less than ninety pounds, clambered over the cliff wall, hammering at stone supports with her heel. She thought Priest could negotiate it. Priest said no. He flexed his ankle; Mary did not challenge him. After two days she had scavenged enough sturdy rope in New Loch, then noosed it to a scrub pine fifty feet above the cave. Rock stubs held when Priest crossed. They had embraced once atop Bull's Hump, but later Priest had disguised impotence with a specious anger. Two days after, as Mary watched, he rode a log over Lenape Falls. Still wet, bleeding from the nose and ears, Priest had made savage love.

Above the fourth landing, a thousand butterflies slept. Priest detached his mask. He scrubbed insect corpses from the mesh with his thumbnail. He loitered. He didn't yet want to disturb them. They were monarchs: upper rinds of wing light reddish brown, white center spots leaded by dark arteries. The wings were shut, harp-shaped. Set in green creeper niches, they seemed eyes of a peacock's tail. Priest inhaled. Then he heard the dogs. He unshuttered creeper, peered over the inner rail, toward the river. At first he was blinded by a contrast of penumbra beneath the viaduct, sunlight beyond. He saw the gnome guardsman trudge: heavy steps. Dogs clothed his body. Languidly he raised arms to shoulder height, some man shrugging on a bulky overcoat. Then the guardsman was down, his form obliterated by feeding dogs. Others waited impatiently; they nipped at haunches of the eaters. Priest watched one dog vomit a tough shred of green fabric. Priest barged upward, breaking the creeper reredos. Butterflies woke. They hurried in front of his face, blinking for him, as though he saw through veined, sun-dazzled lids.

Priest was on the viaduct. Hollow railings had been pushed out, bow chasers salvoing northward into the low jungle. Priest glanced down apprehensively; his heels were braced against the overgrown curbstone bumper. Below, in a playground, the concrete children's wading pool had filled with rain water. A task force of pin-tailed ducks maneuvered on its surface. Priest heard raucous frogs. But for salmon apartment summits, one flagpole, the distant pencil of an old aqueduct tower, the city was featureless. Dogs scrimmaged between upended swings and slides, barking back over their shoulders. Priest had to eat; once off the railing, his fingertips fluttered. He made rigid fists. Where the viaduct was rooted in the primitive granite of Coogan's Bluff, he saw a large public food trough. Priest walked toward it, one block west. Weakness hobbled his shins in creeper surf; he could not raise them. He opened his mask: the process of drawing breath through the mesh seemed expensive. For several moments he watched the six green/gold spouts. Around their splashing, sere creeper leaves cowered; there was no plant food in the E-diet. Priest jerked off his gloves, let them fall, cupped palms. Slight effervescence tickled there, but the liquid died in his hand. It faded as pebbles will, taken from a stream bed. Mary, he recalled, had made banquets of the E-diet. Soup plates, soup. Champagne glasses, champagne. Six courses, as many shaped containers. Priest lapped. He tried not to swallow deeply. The taste was sweet, cloying. He felt a gritty patina form over his teeth. Priest drank three handfuls.

155th Street was humped. Its blunt top rounded two blocks above, at St. Nicholas Avenue; from there it sloped down another two blocks to Riverside Drive. Here the asphalt had been removed with marvelous industry, its black hexagon mosaics repuzzled then into a crude decorative wall. Twenty years before, some neighborhood eco-committee had made an effort to grow flowers in the wide street bed. Priest's feet encountered strip plantings of a rock garden beneath the creeper. He felt stronger now. He guffawed breath out; cheerfulness jiggled in his shoulders. It irritated him. His digestive tract was barren; the drug worked very suddenly in it. If he blinked, Priest's eyes caught a weird, new focus, as though lenses of a different magnification, each slightly astigmatic, were inserted before his vision. He saw a tree. The tree entertained him: he remembered grinning at it. Yet the image left no memory. He had to see it again. Priest yawned, drawing air into his brain. The sun had almost settled behind the Palisades; it traced long building silhouettes across the street. Their shadows seemed enormously cold: he shivered. He thrummed in his nose—brrrrr. But he wasn't cold at all.

Priest noticed a cubical building. Its tall windows were without glass, and around their frames the creeper was singed. Leaves made black fists. The fire had burned recently. Part of a west wall had collapsed outward; here and there an ember emitted smoke curls. Priest saw the building; his eyes, too, were windows. The building returned his glance. With no conscious motive, he walked toward it. Where sidewalk had been, the creeper growth was black, though still perfectly formed. It crumbled to paper ash when he stepped through. Priest saw aluminum letters on the wall: H   SCH   L. He peered over the windowsill. It had been a capacious gymnasium; the wooden floor was ripped up. Boards had been stacked; now the stacks smoldered, afire at their centers. An acrid stench opened his breathing;

91

he knew the smell of seared human hair. Priest snapped his mask shut.

A tall sliver of window had imploded. It lay sideways against the frame, intact. Twilight entered at a freak angle, destroyed translucence, made a mirror of it. Priest watched his anonymous skull, black and sleek, with the abstract death mask of plastic across it. The head nodded. Priest saw the nodding and nodded. Impossibly there seemed to be a time lapse between nod and nod's reflection. Priest wondered who it was. With inept fingers he broke open the snaps of his mask. He saw flat cheekbones, crushed nose, Mongoloid lids. It was not his face. Priest thrust backward, terrified. He fell prone on the cremated, fragile creeper leaves. Ash puffed up around him. Priest stood hurriedly in the spread-eagle imprint of his body. He could recall neither face nor reflected face; he could not recall the cause of his anxiety. He ran in a hampered, low scuttle westward, but the drug soon gentled him. His movements became disorganized. And he laughed.

The street crested, leveled. Priest was sitting: the Chapel of the Intercession awed and surprised him. It was tremendous. At first he could not believe it was man-built. Only the roof peak had surfaced, a bald tonsure in the tousling creeper. He supposed it a natural granite outcropping, but rectangular eye sockets in a tower above the apse had been poked through. He saw flushed sky behind. Priest lay full length in the creeper, one knee up, admiring it, imitating its shape. Priest guessed that this was a church, though he knew only propaganda tales of the Christian faith. Christians ate flesh, drank blood. He sat up, alert. He had sensed figures moving.

At the tower base, nosed into by apse and cloister arcade, he saw a deep graveyard. Dusk, exacerbated by festoons of creeper in the crowded, dead tree boughs, had advanced half an hour there. Priest wanted to see people. He walked to the fence. His head ached—a cost of resisting the drug. Mosquitoes drizzled, draped veil-like, billowing in the gloom. He counted perhaps two dozen figures. They were naked.

Some knelt, pushing forward, drawing back, as his mother had rasped clothes over her washboard. They were clustered, four or five together. Priest stepped through a gap in the railing. Mosquitoes sang, angry electric wires, around his ear-hole mesh. Several men glanced at him, but they were apathetic. Here and there wide turfs of creeper had been uprooted carefully, then folded back on themselves, carpets. To the left he saw four figures on four sides of a shallow excavation. They pushed handfuls of soil in, sifting it patiently for life. Mosquitoes caped their shoulders. Priest walked near. One of the men looked up; his beard around the mouth was caked brown, as though he had been eating dirt. He raised his hands; he offered Priest soil. Priest looked down, then started. He punched at his face, cracking plastic cheekbones. A woman and an infant were sprawled, embraced, in the grave. From groin to feet the mother was shrouded with dirt. Still alive, she shifted her legs slightly, settling covers of a bed. Priest staggered back.

His agitation astonished them. On the slow lens speed of their drugged vision, his running form left a hundred still images. Priest clamped his plastic mouthpiece. He vocalized as he inhaled, screamed into his own throat. He saw the

93

Hudson. By an optical trick it appeared upright, lit from behind, a cyclorama wall beyond two green/black creeper wings at the foot of 155th Street. He musjudged the downslant and his own momentum. He fell, ripped a foot-long divot from the creeper sward. Priest stood. He panted; his mask fogged. He was half a block from the parapets of Riverside Drive. Priest ignored his ankle. His armpits opened as he ran, fingers flat and separated, palms flapping. He stopped in a broad plaza of intersecting avenues. It was brighter there. Slowly now, afraid, Priest crossed to the parapet wall. He unsnapped his mask, gazed north; river wind prised in and blew the mask wide. Priest gasped. His hands tore creeper growth from the wall. He had no hope.

The bridge was down.

HE DREAMED that spasms were in the earth. A dry field buckled; combers of soil and rock attacked his balance. Forms were in process, unstable. Priest awoke; he lay on his back. It was dawn. Kneecaps had folded against his rib cage. Intestines churned in a busy, false peristalsis. He was nauseated. Priest turned his face sideways, into the parapet wall; he lay now where he had collapsed the night before. He whimpered. The spasms evolved in three stages. Paraplegia below the hips: an irresistible nerve reaction that drew knees up, set shivery, hot cramps in thigh and calf muscles. A rough pair of hands palpated his abdomen; the belly surface undulated toward ribs, cresting, troughing, cresting. Then his knees spread. He panted, straining foolishly against the contractions; he had never learned the Natural Digestive Exercises. Hands clapped quickly over his groin. He had almost herniated there; it was a common effect of spasms. He sensed slight moistness between the buttocks. Priest counted to three hundred; at three hundred the convulsions would begin again.

He rested when the spasms were over. Sensitive temporary swellings formed under his armpits, in his groin. The day was clear, but to the southwest cumulus clouds, tall as battle-ships, advanced grandly. Mist wadded the air over Trinity Cemetery. Priest waited, thinking. He had noticed something the night before. It gave him hope; it terrified him. Priest found his stone in the pouch and sucked on it. He sat up. The skin on his palms had begun to jaundice. He stood, supporting torso's weight on the parapet wall. There were corroded lamps at intervals along its rim, two nude sockets suspended in a single axis, a set of scales. Priest looked at the river, postponing certainty. The Hudson was lovely. It was immense: Priest had known the Hudson in its late adolescence, fifty miles upstream near the old Storm King Highway. It was twice as broad here. A travertine path of blue/green reflective plates led across from the just risen sun. Fish simmered near the shore, attracted there by teeming insect life. Priest gobbled breath. He was apprehensive. He had no other option. He turned to look north.

Fear made him nod. Twin-deck roadways of the George Washington Bridge had disappeared. On the New York side, steel and concrete had sheared off exactly: there was no sign of debris in the water. On the Jersey side, breaks were more jagged; falling, the roadway end had bounced once, then caught in the caisson's top. Now it ramped two hundred yards into the water, a ribbon twisted over once. This peninsula was somewhat buoyant; currents eddied briskly around it. But the roadway did not concern Priest. His memory had been accurate. Far above, anchored in top windows of each huge tower, a single cable remained, spanning the Hudson.

It slacked down gradually to a nadir at the river's midpoint. Priest didn't know if he could approach the cable base, but he supposed that access had been provided for maintenance. From twenty-five blocks south, the cable seemed as delicate against the sky as pencil strokes on cloth. Priest turned away, down. He stared at the shattered parallel lanes of the West Side Highway. One stanchion was still upright, supporting a few square yards of elevated highway, and on this pedestal a car had been islanded. Priest cursed: he doubted his courage. He began to walk north.

The asphalt of Riverside Drive had been pulverized. Black powder coned up between the creeper roots—anthills. Priest watched the bridge as he walked. At certain angles past 165th Street, a second strand of cable became visible behind the first. If he could cross to New Jersey before night, Priest would have six days to walk the forty-five miles north. Six days unless Mary was given the pill sooner. Priest feared that: his wife had never resisted the Guard. Two years before, Ogilvy had raped her; Mary had not told Priest. She knew the act was a trap for her husband's anger. There had been no risk of conception; vasectomy was routine, an initiation rite, in the Guard. Throughout, Ogilvy and his two lieutenants had sucked Mary's body, drawing blood up, blotching her with superficial bruises. Though it was mid-August Mary had not gone naked for a week. She made love in the dark. Ogilvy waited expectantly, appearing each day outside Mary's house with his bodyguard. Nothing had happened. Ogilvy hesitated; then he sent Priest a letter. But

97

when Ogilvy arrived the next day, Mary said merely that her husband had gone into the forest. She had been bruised again: the dark blue of Priest's blows contrasted almost handsomely with the stippled red/purple of the guardsmen's sucking. Mary could hardly stand upright, but she had smiled.

He was gone three weeks, hunting without a kill. For his size Priest could move lithely, silently, and he was indefatigable. Once, during twelve hours he had pursued a female deer, following its trail relentlessly, starting it up again and again, demoralizing the animal despite its superior speed. Before dusk it waited for him, flank against an impenetrable grove of hawthorn. It quivered with anxiety, defeated. Priest shut his fingers around the doe's throat. His pressure extruded the long tongue; its eyes bugged. Priest laughed, then he spanked the deer across one buttock. It galloped, staggering, glancing off tree trunks, into the marshland north of Bull's Hump.

A week later, at dawn, the bear attacked him. It was female: he had noted its five-toed spoor for several days, claw marks like incurving candle flames on candles. Fortuitously Priest had intervened between mother and four cubs at a bend called the Elbow of Little Rope River. As he walked north now, Priest remembered the magnificent impetus that had breasted him. It was to this, at last, that he had owed temporary freedom: the kill had assuaged his bitter fury. Big rump upraised, the bear rushed headlong at him, as though overbalanced by an anatomical gravity. Drawn teats ran under it, a centipede's treadmill legs. Her claws had met behind him, had punctured, then had thoughtfully peeled down long shreds of his insect suit over the spine. Priest had been winded, but instinctively he did not pull back, pressing instead toward the bear's chest, face to muzzle, cheek against slaver. They tumbled over and over along an abbreviated incline to the stream bank, both panting with shock at the sudden encounter. The bear urinated in its excitement. Priest's breath gushed up when its weight emptied his lungs. He clung to its pelt, cheating the claws of free play.

Though it was a criminal offense, Priest had not given up his father's hunting knife. He kept the knife in a tree hollow twenty feet above ground. He seldom dared carry it, but now the hilt was against his chest, sheathed by an inside suit pocket. The hilt bruised him when his ribs spread for breath. Priest guessed that the bear was amusing itself: perhaps she had learned that men, upright black animals, no longer cared to defend themselves. The bear snuffled moistly, as if Priest's scent were more alarming than his arms and legs. Priest recalled a first reaction when the bear's shoulders closed on him, when his shoulders met and thwarted that closing. He felt exuberant. It was competition; he craved it.

Movement in his right wrist was circumscribed, yet Priest managed to work his zipper open. The bear had not utilized its jaws; they could not vise Priest's cranium. When jaws nuzzled, he butted at the hard canine teeth, hurting them. He was in pain but not hampered by it. The bear, frustrated, began jostling him side to side pointlessly. Priest would not relinquish his grip on its fur; he protected his vulnerable belly against the bear's belly. He did not shout pain when a claw lodged between ribs. Priest brought the knife out, hilt downward. He was in jeopardy then, for he could have only one chance. He had to aim, to incline his face toward the bear's jaws. The animal sensed this and was ready. Its teeth clamped over his face, crunching the insect mask. The bear's head arched back, masticating, tossing plastic toward its throat, certain that it had flayed the enemy's face of skin. Priest thrust upward, close to his own cheek, both hands on the knife hilt. Its blade skewered through the lower jaw, pinned it to palate above. Claws came free. Unstoppered, blood ran from punctures over Priest's kidneys. He felt its flow. The bear rolled aside, tried to disengage. It wallowed in panic, helpless without powerful jaws. Priest rode the animal's body, sawing downward toward windpipe, until his face and chest were enameled with the hardening blood.

He camouflaged the carcass. For years Priest had not been hungry in the old way. Then he was ravenous: instinct shouted that he compound triumph by eating his victim, but he did not dare—Ogilvy tested his blood once a month for Organic Food Content. Eerily placid, Priest returned to New Loch. The bear's clawing had infected him: he was feverish for a month. Mary knew from delirious yells that he had killed, but the killing had exorcised Priest's anger, and during more than a year he had ignored Ogilvy's taunts. Yet, after all, the least of provocations had brought him to Yankee Prison: two fingers goosing between his buttocks. Priest had hauled Ogilvy into the air by a green scruff of his insect hood. He could still feel Ogilvy's Adam's apple, a big, elusive knuckle under his thumb. When Priest roused from the stunning, his hands were so fiercely locked that finger joints cracked again and again as he flexed them open.

The bridge tower was splendid, immense. Priest stood on a ruined access ramp: explosions had broken it into a staircase, the tiers of a shallow amphitheater. He was scared. Unconsciously Priest imitated the tower's great straddle, palms flat on spread thighs. Lobed, active cumulus clouds flecked with olive, rose on short strings above New Jersey. Rain, Priest thought. It was eight o'clock: he had lost a full hour severing the creeper vine with his teeth. Twice guardsmen had nearly apprehended him in the act. The vine was coiled six times around his chest, under the insect-suit shirt. Priest climbed onto the highest tier level. Thirty years before, a long skirmish had been fought at the Manhattan bridgehead. There was a plaque; battle equipment had been left as a memorial. Tank cannons fired creeper growth. One jet plane's tail section levered under an apartment house at 178th Street and Pinehurst. Artillery bombardments had weakened the span then, though neither faction had wanted to destroy the bridge. After sixteen days the combined Realist and Christian Nihilist guerrilla forces had run out of fuel.

He walked under the tower arch, toward the precipice. As he approached it, Priest's body became afflicted. He aged; he seemed shorter. His knees broke. Shoulders huddled and his chin inclined toward their huddling. The seat of his body jutted backward, ballast. His fingertips felt over the pavement. Then he was on all fours. As he gazed down/over

101

the brink, Priest lay fully prone, arms and legs and fingers spread, a dead man's float. Even prone, vertigo had confused his senses; a burbling voice talked inside his left earhole. He was two hundred feet above the water. Priest could see portions of the bridge roadway, green-yellow, bobbing a yard under the river's surface. He could not watch longer. Priest rolled over onto his back.

The two cables waited above him. They were moored to the northern and southern corners of the tower. On the northern face a third cable drooped down, past him, over the precipice—a vast trunk drawing up water. The two cables had been anchored a few yards below the topmost girderwork. Priest guessed that they were at least two hundred feet above the roadway. He swallowed: the voice in his ear was interrupted by static. Priest could see no safe means of passing from tower structure to cable. He wiped glove palms over plastic temples. A fresh breeze blew: four hundred feet above the Hudson it would be dangerously stronger. There was movement in the cables. Priest knew that his body would want to crawl backward, along the cable's downslant. A headlong approach would terrify him; he could already imagine the dread illusion of overbalancing. Yet he would have to crawl head first. Beyond the midpoint he could never work backward up the long incline to New Jersey. And he could not turn around. Priest began creeping away. He dared not delay. Yet he was unable to stand until he had crawled more than twenty feet from the edge.

Priest chose the southern leg of the tower. It had tremendous geometry: rectangles were stacked, each more than thirty feet tall, each braced corner to corner by a giant X; eight rectangles from roadway to summit. The metal was piebald now, brown/zinc. Areas of old paintwork had bubbled, then cracked open, fragile egg ends. On the tower's inner wall Priest found an unhoused elevator shaft. Six cables dangled down out of an astonishing perspective; above, they were braided together by optical laws. Priest stuffed the mask into his thigh pouch, then retied both bootlaces. The right ankle distressed him. He had overexerted it the day before. The ankle barely fit his boot now; rubber was swollen, the lace holes squinted. He hadn't removed the boot; Priest knew it wouldn't go on again. Priest grasped one cable in his gloved hands, transmitted a shiver of decreasing amplitude two hundred and forty feet up, into the tower's skull. Priest began to climb. He loped up in thirty-foot jaunts. Powerful arms bore the weight of torso and abdomen and thigh; his left heel picked out footholds, stepping from rivethead to rivethead on the X. At the top of each rectangle he rested five minutes, staring only upward, his body hammocked between cable and I beam. For every fifty feet of altitude the wind's velocity doubled. Cables rang, human soprano voices in an empty metal chamber. It was almost nine o'clock.

Priest gazed out, panting. He was on the fifth rectangle, one hundred and sixty feet above street level. His hands burned: shavings of rubber curled from the glove palms. Exactly below the tower arch, on the broken roadway, Priest saw a circle. It was made of bodies, perhaps three dozen. Insect suits were black, but a crimson epaulet marked

103

each shoulder, an insigne of the Northern Lesbian Communes. They sat, feet into the circle. Then legs spread by some ritual instruction and the circle seemed to sphincter out, a lazy, drugged pupil. Priest climbed again. His belly and groin muscles ached as they threw his feet up along the corroded girdering. On the sixth rectangle's top he rested longer. Priest was overheated: chill gusts caused him to shiver. He saw now that the women had shaped a gauntlet. A single figure stepped between. She was naked. She walked out of the gauntlet with the overlarge, adamant steps of a drunkard, toward the precipice. She had time to stride twice in mid air. Then she was gone. Priest gasped. The elevator cable bellied away from the tower. His feet scraped off the I beam. His shoulder bones cracked, gunshots. He hung for several seconds, kicking crazily for the sill. When he stared down again, the circle had begun to re-form.

The last rectangle was smaller. The tower had slimmed at its summit. Priest could see pulley mechanisms of the elevator just above him. He looked out. The metal gridwork, X overlapping X, grouted intricate mosaics of the Manhattan prospect. The sun rayed through a cloud's moving transom, spotlighted a mile-square sector beyond Central Park. The fire still burned; its smoke attached a dark pseudopod to the cumulus clouds above. When the wind blew, it uncovered spiky artichokes of flame. Priest could see the Triboro Bridge towers to the south, but he did not know what they were. Priest inhaled. He let his legs dangle; then, as children pump a swing, he kicked his body in higher and higher arcs toward the I beam. He let the elevator cable go. He legged across the I beam saddle. Testing his will, Priest glanced into the elevator shaft. His reaction was oddly neutral: the confusing perspective of metal crossing, recrossing, was outside his fear's comprehension. For the first time he felt optimistic. He hopped along the girder in modest efforts, pushing up on his wrists, until he had reached the tower's New Jersey face.

The great cable wallowed above him. It was a yard in diameter. Priest stood upright on the girder, hands reaching up toward the X's transept. He climbed its slant, crouched, feet splayed out for balance, yanking with his arms. He crawled over the girder on its inside face and sat in the upper crotch of the X. Standing gingerly, he could now pat the cable's bulged flank with his fingertips. The wind bothered him: its pummeling gusts were erratic in force, in direction. He climbed as high as he could on the X's upper right leg, then stood, holding the top frame of the last rectangle by pinches. The cable bottom was level with his right shoulder. He hung, spine slightly arched outward over the river. Priest flexed his knees, practicing the leap he would have to make. His right ankle buckled, but Priest had no choice then. He could not descend.

Patiently, clutching the girder with alternate hands, Priest shucked off his gloves. He jammed them into his right thigh pouch. Then he transferred papers, stone, mask from vest pockets to left thigh pouch. He would have to crawl on his stomach for hours, across more than half a mile of cable. Priest shuffled several inches higher on the slanted X girdering. He waited for the wind to subside. Curious then, he caressed the cable's surface with his right hand. It was warm, corroded in tiny, slick balls of rust. He brushed there, procrastinating. Priest gazed over his shoulder. Despite its thickness the cable danced above the river; it seemed a child's jump rope just come to rest, full of tiny, dodging motions. The Hudson was featureless as pavement, dark gray, for now the sun had gone in. It was, to Priest, an emblem of annihilation. And he leaped.

Priest's body had surprised him. As he swiveled in mid-air to face the cable, his mind was still conceiving, still preparing the act. He hovered, arms upraised, in mammoth emptiness. Then hands slapped down/over the cable's hump and held, his forehead just above the highest arc of its circumference. Legs kicked. It wasn't enough: his left hand slipped. Priest opened both palms to gather friction from the rusted metal. He did not dare kick again. There was elastic life in the cable and it startled him. The wind toyed with his dangling lower body; gusts pressed his stomach against the cable, then peeled his legs and groin away. His shoulder caps and the insides of his elbows began to ache. Cheek against metal, Priest whimpered, and his ear, hearing fully a half mile, was answered by the roar of resilient metal. In a few seconds, Priest knew, he would fall. The idea, abstracted, was pleasing to him. Priest thought, I will scream then; oh, I will scream. No one can stop my scream. But one eye glimpsed: the huge tower became slim-waisted, plummeting to the roadway, plummeting again to the river. He could not end that way; his body would not consent. He imagined his own fall and it was like death by shrinking. A dot, splashless, gray, absorbed into the gray of that wide slate surface below. He sobbed.

Turning his face cautiously on the corroded flank—cheek/chin/cheek—Priest looked left, then right. Near his right hand there was a raised spine, where sections of sheathing had been riveted together, no more than an inch high. By reaching for it he might lose his tenuous grip. Priest would have to grope quickly, blindly. The wind bellied under him, lifting. He groaned: both hands had slipped downward. He waited until the wind reversed direction. A strong puff shoved at the small of his back, locking chest momentarily against the cable. He squirmed upward, flailing out with his right hand. He dropped. His fingers rushed, gripless, over the spine. Then thumb and forefinger hooked on a rivet. It was a precarious hold. He could not wait; his stamina was going. Priest's hand closed, his entire weight supported on left palm, on right thumb and forefinger. He wrenched up, kicking. The uneven rivet slashed his thumb's ball. But he had made progress; his left toe, hurdling up, had touched the cable's underside. He threw himself upward again and, at apex of lunge, released his precious, pinching hold. His right hand sought wildly and captured a rivet three inches higher. His toe scratched at the rusty cable, then dropped off. The weight of lower body, released suddenly, dislocated cartilage in his shoulders. He gasped. He tasted blood under his tongue. But Priest had advanced upward. Now his head was above the cable's crest; he could see his own hands.

He had to wait for the wind. The cable rolled, a vessel coming about in small, deep swells. Priest needed to hike his left foot up, to create leverage for his lower body. But now the wind opposed him; it crowbarred at his hold. Legs blew backward and their knee joints bent up behind; heels spanked buttocks. Abruptly the wind reversed: Priest felt a boost at his crotch. Desperate, he kicked up again. His right hand closed on the next rivet. His left toe found purchase, held, then pushed up. He was on the cable: in eagerness he almost toppled over the far side. His nails bent, clawing. Then he crushed his body to the cylinder, arms and legs straddling, embracing. Priest fought an eerie sort of unconsciousness. He yawned. He wanted to sleep: his mind was distancing terrible perceptions. Then he saw and understood the river. Unimaginable height had turned its softness to granite. He saw and understood the treacherous rope he would have to cross. Now, momentarily safe, Priest was afraid for the first time. He began to tremble. Knees and elbows beat at the sheathing. His tongue curled throatward: teeth chattered until he thought they would break off at the roots.

The sheathing was packed with sound. It boomed into Priest's flattened ear as wind shouldered against the cable: thunderous pealing of shaken metal sheets. Priest gazed west, down the incline. Long perpendicular waves traveled at him from the New Jersey shore: they grew in height over mid-river, then slackened, yet were powerful enough near the tower to toss his hips a full inch off the sheathing when they crested. His legs lay slightly higher than his head: Priest had an appalling sense of headlong overbalance. There was great turbulence over the river. The wind chopped at him sedulously, chiseling here and there under his body. He could not anticipate it. The cumulus clouds had become thunderheads; they opened to show black inner cores. The cable was in agony, unguyed by its vanished roadway. Priest did not think it would hold many more days.

Gingerly, unwilling to raise his torso more than two inches above the cable, Priest zipped open his insect-suit front, then uncoiled the creeper vine. Using teeth and the fingers of his right hand, he knotted the thinner vine end around his left wrist. Then he dropped it over the cable's southern flank. It dangled, jiggling in eddies of wind. He swung the vine through gradually increased pendulum arcs, waiting for a southwesterly gust to help him. Then he whipped the vine upward. It curled around the cable's underbelly and slapped the back of his groping right hand. He paused, tried again. His fingers caught the thick end, but they were stiff and lacerated from their punishing hold on the rivet-head. He bungled the grip. Priest hesitated, panting. He felt incontinent; he pushed down on his empty bowels. There was a twinge from some unnoticed strain between his legs. He cheated toward the right so that he could judge with his eyes. This time he pinned the creeper vine under his palm and drew the slack securely to him.

He used his knees, rising up, lunging a foot or fifteen inches forward, slackening the vine's grip, sliding it ahead. Wind slugged at his exposed flank as he hunched above the cable on all fours. His knees were chafed raw by the rusty, pitted metal surface. He progressed a hundred feet; then the vine caught. It hooked below on a bracket stump:

one of the sheared support anchors that had held the bridge roadway up. He released the vine from his right hand. He slithered six inches past the obstruction. Head pressed against the metal, Priest began to whip the vine up to his right hand again. Fifteen times in three hours he was halted by the vine; fifteen times he stubbornly repeated the freeing process. As he crawled downward, the cable's undulations increased. It sidewindered; simultaneously it rose and fell. The bucking turned vicious: at times he was secured only by the vine. He became seasick and retched aridly. The material of his insect suit had worn to tissue; then the insides of his thighs were naked. Then his skin began to wear away. It was necessary now to predict the rollers, to watch them form below the New Jersey tower. He dared push forward only in the troughs. And the terrific crashing grew, reverberated as he neared the river's center: a thousand steel vertebrae slamming together.

It began to rain. Drizzle glossed the sheathing; particles of rust floated in a slick, superficial colloid. It lubricated the front of Priest's insect suit. There was no friction. He tobogganed down the cable slant without effort, twenty feet at a time. Once, he skidded the full length of a single tubular sheath, stopped abruptly as the vine snagged below. Explosive drops pelted down. He could see whitecaps on the river; they seemed spread wings of gulls. The city had been enveloped; mist bubbled down/over the brink of the Palisades. The rain continued; then the heavens seemed to inhale, a great diaphragm held taut. It was suddenly cold. And hail fell. The cable howled with shrill, infernal hammering percussions. Ice bits were big as silver dollars, their rims clipped and lumpy. Now the wind was single-minded; it blew at fifty miles an hour from the southwest. The cable bellied outward, a hammock swinging. Priest grasped the vine fearfully. Twice the cable arced so high that he was suspended sideways above the Hudson. His left ear and temple bled—opened by the hailstones. Then a bolt of lightning struck the northern cable. Blue glows flooded its length from tower to tower. Priest thought it was beautiful and expected death.

He was stalled there for twenty minutes. Then sunlight barged through the last, ragged sheets of drizzle. A fleet rainbow leaped from the Palisades; it shot between retreating buttocks of a cloud. At once the cable began steaming. Its insane gallop subsided to regular, profound swells. Priest unhooked the vine, secured it again; started edging forward. By two o'clock he noticed the first true upslanting: he had accomplished half the distance. But it was difficult now to move forward. The metal was still slick in places; gravity worked against his weight. Pain in raw inner thighs had paralyzed his calves and shins. Yet Priest felt that the worst was past. The grim sensation of overbalancing had gone, and the cable's hill protected him somewhat from wind. His vine caught. Priest lay one ear flat on the metal sheathing and dropped it free.

He heard groups of sound. They punctuated the monotonous, long grinding of metal against metal. Priest clutched the vine end. He lashed it around his right wrist, but hesitated before moving. He was puzzled; he pressed his other ear to the metal. He identified a crude rhythm: scrape, chunk-chunk, scrape, repeated. Not loud, yet with clear persistence. Priest prodded knees into the cable, ascended several feet. He stopped to listen again. Then he jerked onto all fours, nearly upsetting balance. He cursed under his breath. There it was; he gazed up along the cable slope. A head and a pair of shoulders; they were moving toward him. Priest pounded at the sheathing in fury, but the other figure did not see him. It moved relentlessly, cheek to metal, perhaps a third of the way across. Two hundred feet from Priest. And Priest lunged upward; he meant to contest every yard of the cable.

They almost butted head to head. It was a young boy, no more than seventeen years old. He ducked backward; he cowered. The boy appeared incredulous, astonished; he hadn't seen Priest before. Wind stiffened his hair, long, black, and lifted it straight up as if on a hinge at the part line. His nose was beaked; it had flaring nostrils that pulsed open and shut, fearful. Priest saw no vine or rope. The boy was trusting balance; he had started down after the thunderstorm. His eyes crossed, then closed. He burrowed face into the hump of his right shoulder. Corrosion had rouged one cheek. Priest mouthed, "Back up. Go back." The boy wet his lips; there was a stone in his mouth. He had not understood. Exasperated, Priest tried to indicate with his shoulders: yet it was foolish, he could never back to the New Jersey tower. Apologetically then the boy extended one hand to catch Priest's left wrist and forearm. He began chatting with fingertips. Priest yanked his wrist away; the boy chased it. From fierceness in the grip, Priest guessed his terror. Then

112

the hand relaxed. Priest made the slash sign, "No"—he could not comprehend. But the boy interpreted his response as a threat.

Priest lipped, "Climb over me. Climb over me." His thumb, held down by the vine, jabbed in half circles toward the New York shore. But the boy was apparently unconscious. His small mouth gaped amazement. Gaped, remained open as his eyes were open, stunned, immobile. Priest was sickened: he knew suddenly, vividly how the boy would look in death. Priest tried to smile encouragement. Then wind rolled the boy's long hair down and he was eyeless, masked above the stupid mouth. The cable reawakened. Long swells began to snap off at their crests, each a shuddering, quick drop. The boy's slim rear hopped, hopped again: he slid several inches forward. Priest backed reluctantly. He wanted to strike out, to close that imbecile mouth, but the vine occupied both hands. A black cape swirled from the Palisades. It dipped once, the dip repeated through several hundred yards. Priest saw a crowded flock of sparrows. They furrowed under the cable, and, just beneath, a staccato, indignant chirping spattered up. They were startled by the presence of men in their element; formations became disordered below him. But their twittering had aroused the boy. He lifted himself slightly on elbows, turned his face so that hair poured down/over his left ear. One eye emerged. Priest said again, "Climb over me. Climb over me." In agitation he dropped the vine from his right hand. Deliberately then he made several passes with his arm, backward, over one shoulder. The boy understood at last and was dismayed.

113

He shook his head. He was afraid. Priest covered the boy's left wrist, tapped: "Please, please, please." The boy shook his head again. Furious, Priest grasped slack of hood behind the boy's nape. He pulled toward him, but the boy lay flat then, a dead weight. Priest released him. Despondent, he rasped his forehead against the sheathing.

Abruptly the boy pushed up with both arms. He sat astride the cable. Hands prayed over his chest; dry blood was encapsulated beneath each fingernail. Priest became concerned. He mouthed, "Get down. Get down." Wind seized its opportunity, but the boy's reflexes were good. He slipped upsetting gusts, right shoulder shrugged against his ear. He saw beyond Priest; hands dropped to shelter his groin. Priest motioned him forward. The boy tilted left: he did not advance. Once, then, he shook his head, but it was a larger negative, not intended for Priest alone. The mouth closed; the eyes closed. Lazily he toppled left, over the cable's edge, legs still astraddle. Priest lunged foolhardily. His fingers rapped the side of one instep as it left the sheathing. In fetal position, tumbling, the boy plunged down. At once he was annihilated by distance, a mote dissolving through colorless backgrounds. And, in obedience, he fell without sound. Priest snapped his head back. He howled, affording a human voice to death.

Priest lay on his back below the New Jersey tower. It had been full night for two hours. Even a light breeze stung his flayed inner thighs. Glossy chaps of dried blood had formed there; rubber fabric was grafted to it. He could not walk

114

normally. Priest's eyes were open. Through the uncontaminated atmosphere he saw random seedings of nebulae, more clustered as they were farther from the earth. Water below him rebounded from the half-submerged roadway island, and its rushing, and the stars, and his extremities made remote by lassitude, these were all interpenetrable things. He might have been any of them. Priest sat up, disturbed. Mosquitoes started away, then resettled on his face. The insect mask had cracked in half during his descent from cable to roadway. Rain had not doused the fires. Across the river he could see wide glows that expanded and contracted noiselessly, lungs of the city. He stood, wrenching up on girderwork. He stepped forward with his heels wide, stiff at shoulders and hips and knees. Cicadas whirred: their sound was hot, a good conductor. Priest staggered; he needed a place to sleep. Over high foreheads of blasted rock, a full moon rose. He could see fairly well. The tollbooths in their plaza, roofless, plastic-sided, had served as greenhouses. They were congested with vegetation. Priest stumbled west on Route 4. Dandelions had won there and milkweed and fireweed; the Canada thistles chafed thorny leaves through his spread crotch. His right ankle had swollen frighteningly; liquids sloshed in it. The boot would have to be cut off.

The left lane of Route 4 had eroded; it was a ravine several feet deep. Now modest rillets moved in it, supporting a new ecosystem: there were frogs, crayfish, a stand of water willow. Its sewers had become strangled and, in spring thaws, water, extravasating, rivered toward Overpeck Creek along the highway bed. Moonlight was preservative: Priest

115

accepted the roadside civilization of thirty years before. The motels, the filling stations, the drive-ins had not been bull-dozed. They looked whole, clean. The creeper had not been sowed in New Jersey. Priest blew upward, lower lip pro-trusive, chasing mosquitoes and no-see-ums from his eyes. By fierce rote he reiterated the chant of eight hours, though now it was irrelevant and confusing. One-two, three. One-two, three. Up on elbows, slide vine ahead, kick. He hurt at ankle and thigh and shoulder. This did not dishearten him. Priest had great capacity for pain; it was his best talent. He stayed on the right verge on Route 4. A three-story motel appeared pristine, attractive, but he knew that most buildings had been securely boarded up. And some, on the highways, had been booby-trapped by fanatics just after the Decree.

Priest saw the shell. This same emblem had turned easily, obverse and reverse identical, one rotation every five seconds, above Sebastian Priest's filling station. Young Priest had once imagined the station and the farm and his own body to be parts of some dioramic mechanical toy, the sign its key, winding down. He walked into the front plaza. Squat, an-thropomorphic gas pumps had toppled; they lay side by side, faces down, as though dormitoried. There was a cliff of red-dish stone, black now against the clear sky, two hundred feet behind the main building. Priest tried the door but it was warped shut; wood dust of termites showered on him from the eaves. He shuffled away. An air pump, hose still looped around its bracket, had been riveted to the building's corner. The hose cracked into half circles when Priest touched it.

116

The machine's handle would not turn. He remembered the games he had played with Sebastian Priest's hose: bubbling in the tire tank, a submarine periscope; air under the shorts of a friend momentarily puffed out cloth buttocks. He kicked pieces of rubber on the asphalt. A hand touched his shoulder.

Priest pivoted around, insucking breath, fists prepared. His ankle gave; he knelt unwillingly. A spry, thin man stood in shadows of the building wall. His beard was braided; several dozen clinking medals had been knotted into it. He backed two fingers against his forehead, a V, the accepted sign of peace. Priest shrugged irritably. The man stepped forward. He was nude, his skin ghastly in the moonlight. Priest ignored the peace sign. The man grinned. He inclined slightly to cup one hand over Priest's genitals: the sensitivity greeting. It had evolved from encounter-group psychology in the 1980s; established by Decree at the century's end. It was meant to show trust; put your most vulnerable parts at the mercy of strangers. In reluctance, for Priest loathed this intimacy, he flicked fingertips across the man's penis. It was half erect.

The man laughed without sound. His legs were curved severely at the shin: big toes pigeoned tip to tip. He might otherwise have been tall as Priest. He took Priest's arm tactfully, began to converse inside it. Priest said no, then gestured at his mouth. It was too dim there for lip reading. The man hesitated. He started to draw Priest toward him, pointing behind the garage. Priest disengaged his arm; he was suspicious. The man mimed "Please," hands in a cup under his chin. Priest did not want involvement, but he

117

needed new insect-suit pants, a new mask. The man disappeared into the darkness toward the cliff; a fragile tinkling was shaken from his beard. Priest followed, legs wide, soles scraping: as when, a five-year-old child, he had played daddy in Sebastian Priest's overlarge, broken workshoes.

They crossed a marshy field. Water swarmed into their deep footprints. Priest closed hands over his face. Skin of cheeks and lips was tumid with insect poisons. Between spread fingers he saw the man bend. He had found a discarded insect suit and from one thigh pouch he removed a death capsule. He pretended to swallow it, then offered Priest the capsule. Priest refused. The man approached. His hips ground, insect suit rubbed across bare teats; the effeminate motions, carried through crooked calves, were grotesque. He touched Priest's thigh. Priest frowned: perfunctorily he slugged the man beneath one shoulder. His fist, withdrawn, was wet with insect corpses. The man backed; he rubbed his arm. He smiled nonetheless, pointed. Priest saw a roomy grave. There were two dead men in it. One knelt, inclined forward on arms and cheek, nude buttocks upraised. The second man clothed him, stomach and groin over back and hips. His lips were open; Priest read noises of pleasure on them.

The man raked one hand through his beard. He sat on the grave's rim; let his feet dangle. He winked at Priest, beckoned. Priest smiled: he was tolerant, but shook his head. The man hassocked heels comfortably on a set of buttocks below him. Priest picked up the insect suit, acted

118

out giving. The man agreed. An insect mask was attached to the hood. Priest popped it off and snapped the mask onto his own hood. It smelled of perfumes. The man watched him, thoughtfully milking his penis. Priest backed away. The man slid into his grave, toes wide as if testing cold water.

North of the Shell station, behind it, a hill had been encarcerated. It was two hundred feet in diameter, sixty feet high. Frames of a tall fence fanned inward. Priest stepped onto the springy wirework. In moonlight, surfaces glistened. The hill was metal, a charnel avalanche of tractor-trailer cabs. They had been piled without dignity on forehead and jaw, upended on cranium pates. Soil had been spread over the hill, but rain and wind had skinned it off. Near the base one cab lay upright, just slightly nodded at its hinging, some elephant about to perform a headstand. Roof and hood were buckled by the tires of another cab stacked atop. Priest stripped turf sideburns from the driver's window. Then, using a corroded jack handle, he knocked out two jagged glass fangs. Priest slithered through the window.

The seat's flesh had rotted out. Soil sifted through its open skeleton of springs. The sleeping compartment above/behind him was crushed down. Priest's head ached. He hung his new insect suit around the window frame. In both elbows an involuntary mechanism took control of his hands, opened and closed them. He wrung fingers, slapped his palms against the roof. With one glass fang Priest cut his insect-suit pants off. Scabs cracked when he peeled the crusty rubber free. Blood seeped again. He was panting crazily:

119

bent double in the seat, his diaphragm had panicked. He took the left boot off, then slashed his right boot along its Achilles tendon. There was no pain in the ankle; sensation, when he touched the sole, was perhaps in his finger, perhaps in his foot. He did not investigate further. Naked, Priest leaned back. After a few seconds he began to shake convulsively. In darkness, without reference, the truck cab had contracted long, nauseating undulations from the cable. Priest tore aside the insect-suit curtain, saw fragments of moonlight, and steadied his perspective on them. He was stiff with tension; he could not sleep. Priest closed uncertain palms on the steering wheel.

Instinctively then, he pinched a sparse forelock of his hair. Priest recognized the gesture. It was his father's salute, his father's hair: eaving over it, the brim of an antique baseball cap, blue sun-bleached white, six metal grommets exhaling around the crown. Priest turned the wheel. It moved generously, no longer attached to the steering works below. He groped for the accelerator. It was under dirt; he excavated it with his left foot. Priest's fingers turned, pushed, switched across the dashboard. He produced an experimental sound, mmmm. The sound of a child seated on his father's lap thirty-five years before, in youth that was, as well, a different age of man's time, the old robin's-egg-blue wrecker rushing ahead, though caught in Sebastian Priest's garage. For several minutes he drove through another dimension. He began to sob and was astonished and ashamed and pleased, for Priest could not recall crying since he had become a man. Then he was no longer astonished: in his nape all the taut cables of that day broke—he heard a distinct noise at his mastoids—and whipped out fiercely, exploded by their tension. Priest slept with one cheek on the round horn button.

HE COULDN'T WORK the boot on. Liquid traveled under his right instep, bleaching skin from purple to white where it moved. Tires came through the broken windshield. With his glass knife Priest carved off a five-inch piece of tread. Patiently, though it was now well past dawn, he bored eyeholes in the rubber with a nail, strung bootlaces through, then between his fattened toes; constructed a rudimentary sandal. It was humid in the cab. Outside, the crane flies swarmed. The air above him jiggled as if shot through with heat waves. They seemed to cartwheel backward, lanky, bumpkin mosquitoes, regulated by some nebular logic. They flurried onto him. Priest found a five-foot length of aluminum tubing, a cane. He swathed his bare ankle with the elastic bandage, then limped toward the highway. It was perhaps seven miles, he thought, to the junction of Routes 4 and 17. Priest hoped to reach Paramus by nightfall.

There was occasional traffic. Pairs of guardsmen patrolled on jittery bicycles. In Indian file the anonymous faces of a lesbian commune passed him, walking south. He mastered the cane's rhythm: hit earth with metal tip as right ankle accepts weight; push off with right arm; hurdle cane ahead.

Most highway overpasses had collapsed; he was forced to make expensive detours. The sun came out. Priest left his mask ajar to dissipate condensation. In the parking lot of a gutted furniture store three dozen people waited with jugs and bottles near a public fountain. Priest was hungry, but he meant to walk another full day before eating. Chafed areas on his thighs had begun to suppurate; the new insect-suit pants were constrictive. Yet he felt exuberant. On the cable he had bluffed old fears. He remembered the doctor in Yankee Prison and laughed, blowing cheeks out, muting sound in their skin. He rehearsed his account of yesterday for Mary. She knew his fear and would be amazed.

Route 4 crossed broad swamplands near the Hackensack River. Priest walked into a twilight of insects; the sun had collapsed, was shrunken. Pigeons and crows in flocks, solitary jays, had gorged themselves flightless. The roadbed was gray/white, oily with their excrement. Under the reeds, cats, perhaps several hundred of them, dashed into quick feather explosions, wolfed down bird flesh. The air reported small deaths by violence. Staring upward, Priest imagined himself on a seabed, fathoms below the turbulent surface. Life registered in blurs, only the darning needles and a few hummingbirds attained the great speed of inertia. Every ten steps Priest scraped his breathing mask clear. Mosquitoes stung through his suit, indifferent to the repellent greases impregnated in it. Priest ground his teeth: he abhorred the sound. He wanted to answer it. And there were bees.

He could not see to avoid them. Their clumped weight bore down burdock and thistle heads. Telephone poles,

cheesy with wood rot, oozed beards of them. The bumblebees swung below their small wings. Yellow jackets stared
into his mask. They could easily sting through his rubber.
Priest owed his child to bees. A year before, he had been
stung in the testicles. Priest had become habituated to pain,
but this was the worst. Had he dared touch his hardened
scrotum, Priest would gladly have torn it from his groin. For
two weeks he had been paralyzed below the hips, afflicted
by strange convulsions. He supposed it had made him im-
potent, but Mary was patient, used to Priest's fierce, suicidal
urges. She had gently coaxed his member, ignoring it, surprising it. They had decided not to have children: Mary had
suffered two dangerous miscarriages; it was not a world that
understood children. But Priest's manhood had resumed un-
expectedly; they had made love without contraception. The
time of the miscarriages had come, had passed. Before he
was taken away, Priest had felt life in her.

Route 4 was barricaded. Locusts washed across it, moving
southeast with the wind. Their gray, triangular bodies re-
paved the highway bed. Swarms would flutter out of the
mass, striped underbellies showed beneath wings, reams of
newsprint riffled. A guards platoon waved Priest left, across
country: he would have crushed too many locusts. Vegetation had been denuded in a mile-wide swathe to the northwest; Priest walked from summer through the last days of
autumn. His detour squandered an hour. It was two o'clock:
he had travled more than five miles since morning. Priest
returned to Route 4 by a forested suburban avenue. He
was tired. Sharp edges of the aluminum tube cored his glove

palm. There had been a treetop fire of great intensity. Candelabra branches were charred, leafy with ash, though undergrowth and trunks had not been harmed. House roofs were black and showed rafters. The siding was curled out. Yet the interiors, though warped by melting, had not caught fire. Priest sat to rest in the yard of a low ranch house.

A woman with one small child crossed toward the house. The child was a girl, perhaps five years old. She had outgrown her insect suit. They were no longer manufactured; it was impossible to find children's sizes. The band of flesh at her waist was purulent with insect bites. Mosquitoes circled there. She had no mask, but held a cloth between bare hands over her face. The woman was blond: unkempt, dirty strands appeared at the join of hood and mask. She was tall. Priest assumed she was at least his age. Scoop seat of pelvis ridged assertively through her tight insect suit. She noticed Priest, paused. Then she walked toward him. The girl child did not follow at once. Irritably, with thumb and forefinger, the woman vised her daughter's nape. The child stumbled forward. The woman snapped open her mask.

Priest hiked up on the cane. He undid his mask: it was a courtesy of the times. She smiled; she had once been handsome. The child squatted, watched them between fingers. The woman took three overlong strides toward Priest. In her fine hips there were downward rotations, an ambulating *contrapposto*. She had large breasts: Priest stared at them; mammary development was rare since the E-diet. She halted, but her torso did not respond fully, seemed to overshoot the pedestal of her hips. She smiled. She might have been

125

his sister: sloped cheekbones, eyes slanted to a squint. Her mouth was broad and never closed. She had sharp canines, but the lower jaw appeared slack. Wrinkles worked out from her mouth corners, from her eyes. Matted hair, caught in fringes of the hood, put muttonchops on her cheeks. She performed the sensitivity greeting; she elaborated it, judging Priest's size with her fingers. He was embarrassed and angry. Priest reciprocated; he squeeed her left breast. The woman laughed, pushed eagerly into his grip. She tapped under Priest's forearm, but he shook his head. She translated the movement of his lips; her own lips imitated simultaneously, a young child first reading. Her breath smelled honeyish; her skin had yellowed. Priest knew that she was heavily drugged. The woman mouthed,

"You can't talk with fingers? Are you too stupid?"

"Yes," Priest mouthed. "I'm too stupid." He limped away. The woman pulled at his elbow.

"Don't go. I like stupid men." She smiled. "I like stupid men with good bodies. Your legs are straight. You have something between them." She pointed toward the ranch house. "My home is there. I want to get laid. I'm tired of playing with myself. Yes? You're not too stupid to understand that?"

"I understand. No."

"Queer?"

"No."

"Don't be so angry. You grit your teeth. Your teeth are terrible. Come inside with me. I'm going to die now." She

126

extracted a capsule from her thigh pouch. "I don't want to face the night again. I'm too alone in the night."

"I have to see my wife. I haven't seen her in months. I've been in prison."

"Yes. I can believe it. You would go to prison." She kissed him. Priest shrank his tongue away from the sugars in her spit. "Your wife won't mind."

"You have a child. It's not a good thing."

"I'll make her wait outside."

"No."

"Yes. For God's sake—one hour. Your wife can give me one hour. I'll make you happy."

The woman unzipped her insect-suit bodice. Fat yellow breasts clung together, ostrich eggs in a sand hollow. They were netted with blue veins. Mosquitoes infested her at once; the nipples were erected by their stinging. She undressed one of Priest's hands, cupped it on her right breast, then moved her shoulders, rotating, against his palm. Priest looked at the child. The woman zipped up irritably, catching Priest's wrist. In the tight, flyless codpiece she saw that he was aroused.

"Come with me. Quick. Be quick." She pushed him toward the house. Priest resisted. "I haven't had a man, not for months. You know what I do?" It was hard to read her lips, the wet tongue slurred over them. "I cut a hole, a tiny hole in my pants. Right there." She pressed her mons veneris. "And I lie in the grass. And I let the bugs eat me. They have a feast." She pushed him again. "Come, I want you."

"No. I can't."

"Bastard. Son of a bitch. You'll be dead in a few days. What are you saving it for?"

"The child's father. Where is he?"

"Dead. Dead." The girl watched them, eyes wide above her cloth yashmak. Her hair was cropped short. Hair cutting, nail paring were forbidden. Priest thought it had been the typhoid epidemic. "She bothers you? Is that it?" Priest shrugged. He picked up his cane. "Wait. Just wait. I'll take care of her." She waved the child forward.

The girl's hands prayed: a sign of obedience. Priest saluted hello and smiled. The woman kissed her daughter on the rubber hood's pate. The child flinched. Clumsily the woman groped in her right thigh pouch. Turning to Priest she mouthed, "That nice man says you bother him." She tapped inside the child's wrist. Frightened, the girl dropped hands and cloth away from her face. With strong fingers then, the woman pried through her daughter's cheeks, opened jaws, pushed the capsule in. Priest almost shouted: he moved suddenly. His nails scraped along gums behind the child's lower lips, raked the capsule out. Its gelatin case had not begun to dissolve. He hurled it toward the blackened fire grate of branches above him. The woman rammed him across the chest with her elbow. Then she staggered sideways and fell. The child's tongue, knowing only the second taste of its life, dug with curiosity in her mouth.

"Whore." Priest said. "Dirty whore."

"Why?" The woman laughed. She lay sprawled. Her legs spread slowly. She scoured her lower back in the pavement dust, as if drying it with a towel. "Why? She has to die. We all have to die."

"Not yet."

"You like children?" The woman produced a second capsule from her pouch. Priest had not understood the question. Her head was nodding. "You like children?"

"Yes. They are alive. I like things alive."

"You like her?" The sun went in. She stared upward, torso balanced on elbows.

"Get up. Take her inside. The insects are eating her."

"Such a good man. You do like her." She held the capsule between thumb and forefinger. She lay it on her tongue. Swallowed it. "I give her to you. Take her. She's yours."

She wrenched insect-suit pants down below her knees. The rubber legs made tourniquets at her calves; skin bulged above. With one hand she drew out a crude wooden dildo, shaped like the letter J. It had been painted red. She wedged down, then meat-hooked it under her groin. Priest was astonished. The woman began to grind her lower body against friction, mouth in a round howl. Priest stepped forward; he screened her from the child. The legs came up, fettered, sack racing in the air. Priest shut the child's eyes. He picked her up. Thin chest against shoulder, he began hobbling toward Route 4. Behind him, the woman hurried her business. But she had no co-ordination, and death, a male, was faster.

Priest could not understand what he had done. Fists met behind his neck, but the child made no attempt to support its slight weight. Her face was edged sideways between his

129

collarbone and his lower jaw. He could not carry her while mitigating the shocks to his ankle. She would cost him hours. Priest held her shallow buttocks, and the snub coccyx pushed through to his palm. After several hundred yards, exasperated by his own foolishness, Priest set her down. She squatted on a broken curb, fingers across cheeks. Festering insect bites knobbed the backs of her hands, some thick as second knuckles. Priest's own mask was several sizes too large for her hood. He unwrapped his elastic bandage and sashed it twice around her raw midriff. She did not respond. Children in this last generation had the stupid patience of senility. He peeled her hands off, unsnapped his mask. She was not attractive: buck teeth; bushy masculine eyebrows; jowls laddered with dark hair. Her father's child, Priest thought.

"Can you read my lips?" Priest saw that it was hopeless. She had never heard human speech; she could not recognize the words. Priest pounded his left knee in frustration. Out of thrift, he had saved the torn insect-suit pants. He ripped them in half at the crotch. He tied one leg around her head above the eyebrows, the other below her cheekbones. The eyes, isolated between two black strips, disturbed him. He had not noticed them before. Blue, fierce, deep: eyes of some animal imprisoned by its own passivity. Yet the body remained listless. Priest jammed the naked, unresponsive left hand into a side pocket. But her right hand resisted. It caught his wrist and tapped: he understood the common phrase, "Thank you." Priest nodded, shrugged. Then they began walking north.

A wide shopping plaza had returned to the earth. Dirt ramps had been bulldozed up against the department-store walls, stepped Inca pyramids now. The cultivated gardens were gone. Dandelions and fireweed monopolized the soil ramps. Thirty years before, this had been the new government's first showplace. A channel had been excavated from Saddle River. It filled an ornamental lake that spread across the cracked asphalt of parking lots, across the highway bed, lapping under the bluff where once Route 17 had overpassed Route 4. The lake was congested with ducks: mallards, mergansers, pintails, Canada geese. Priest had been hearing their barked noise, strange applause, for ten minutes. The lake shore was tufted with legless, compact bodies. Squadrons landed in the water, heels out, wings scraping backward. Priest had to rest.

It was nearly six o'clock. For two hours they had traveled north, the child shuffling behind at the end of Priest's arm. Duck sounds intrigued her now; she visored the rubber blindfold up. Priest was in pain. He looked at his right ankle with frightened loathing. Insects had eaten there. His toenails had grown purple/blue cuticles; they had almost been enveloped. The child began pointing excitedly. Drake mallards dueled near their feet, hissing, cranky. The glossy emerald necks riposted and parried. Quacking clattered. Ducks scooted between big dandelions, rocking from side to side. Priest sat. The drakes carried their squabble over his shins, unintimidated. Still on her feet, the girl bent at hips; she made circumspect, formal stroking motions. She glanced at Priest for permission. A brown female backed from her

131

fingers; it nipped, then preened clamly, grudgeless. Priest opened his mask. The girl chatted against his forearm. Priest shook his head, pointed toward his mouth. She misunderstood, nodded, smoothed her stomach: she was hungry. Priest cursed. He noticed a public fountain at the lake's edge, where fallen segments of overpass had left a rubble archipelago in the water. Priest judged the sun. He slashed no against the girl's arm. With her inconsequential body weight the spasms would start an hour after drinking. He couldn't afford to stop. She formed an interrogative with her hands. Priest indicated by elaborate, silly pantomimes that she would have to wait. The girl nodded agreeably, but she didn't understand why.

Across the lake, above summit horizons of a pyramid, Priest distinguished movement. Unnatural, flat greens were separated out of vegetative greens, motived progress out of the wind's purposeless combing. Two guardsmen walked bicycles down/over/down giant soil stair treads, toward the shoreline. At first he wanted to run. He closed his identity inside the mask. Then Priest reconsidered. With a level motion of his hands he told the child to remain. The guardsmen had begun hauling their machines around the lake margin. Priest's hobbling crowded ducks; nesting females popped up on thin legs, suddenly forced plants. Priest waved, but when nearer he realized that the guardsmen were too young. They would not know speech. He opened his mask, mouthed, "Can you help me?" One guardsman, gold chevrons of a First Monitor on the left biceps, doored open his mask irritably. Without fluence he said,

"Speak hand speak." He presented the inside of his arm. Priest patted chest, thighs, as though rummaging pockets, held up empty palms, a sign of his ignorance. The faceless junior guardsman rapped his own temples, mocking, but the First Monitor pointed toward Priest's identity pocket. He corroborated the photograph; checked Priest's serial number against a roster of wanted men. Priest became agitated: this had been a mistake. He glanced back. The child had not moved; she played now, to the lap in a foam of duck wings. The guardsman slid a pad from saddlebags on his bicycle. Its pages were fragile, old; dog's ears broke off, fluttered, chips of yellow paint. He wrote,

"You have been in prison." Priest nodded. "What was your crime?"

Priest took the pencil. "I spoke. In anger."

"Why are you here? This is far from your home."

"I return from prison. I was let out to die." The First Monitor read. Priest pointed to the girl, scrawled, "Her mother is dead. I found her on the road. I can't take her home with me. Is there someone to care for her?"

The First Monitor thought, handed the pad to his partner. The junior guardsman opened his mask with practiced deliberation. Priest's head dodged back; he was horrified. A hole had been ripped out of the man's face. His mouth corner was brutally extended left, gashed through the cheeks, to jaw hinges. Turned in profile, his side molars were front teeth, grinning under scar tissue and sparse fuzz of the cheek's beard. He produced a plastic case, selected one capsule from it. He offered the capsule to Priest. Priest frowned. The

133

junior guardsman wrote, "She has to die. You can kill her—
or we will." Priest took the pencil.

"I will do it. She trusts me."

"We will watch you."

The junior guardsman smiled: the smile axed open his
head. He was not ashamed of his grotesqueness: he knew
its useful force. Priest turned around. The girl sat fifty yards
away. A drake had fitted itself into her lap. Its breast
cradled over arm crook; the neck slithered down to peck.
The girl's face was pressed into its feathers. Priest accepted
the capsule. He wrote,

"It will take time. I must dig a grave." The junior guardsman nodded. For a moment he chewed the pencil with
gruesome negligence between naked back teeth. Priest could
see his uvula.

"We will help you. The earth is soft here."

Priest's fingers closed over his aluminum cane, but the
First Monitor intervened. He tapped along his subordinate's
arm. They argued. The junior guardsman's face was mute;
Priest watched the man's tongue flop lazily. The junior
shrugged finally. He gave Priest one capsule. The First
Monitor wrote,

"We cannot wait. What is your route to New Loch?"

Priest could not lie: there was only one convenient highway. He pointed to the bluff, north along Route 17. The
First Monitor wrote, "That is our patrol station. Report
to us at the old Paramus bus term. Tomorrow morning. Bring
the child's insect suit as evidence." Priest nodded. "You un-

134

derstand?" Priest nodded. "We have your serial number. You will be watched from here to New Loch."

The First Monitor walked his bicycle ahead, mounted. Its rear tire was spangled with blue patches. The patches circled, blue, blue, blue, then the speeding tire was wholly blue, colored by a stroboscopic illusion. The junior guardsman did not move. He had seen the reflex in Priest's hand. He leaned forward, confiscated the aluminum cane. Priest protested: he boosted his ankle up, hopping. The guardsman's hacked face opened once, closed but did not close. He chopped downward and the cane cut Priest across the left shin. He pedaled away, the aluminum tube held as a javelin above his shoulder. Near the lake's edge he hurled it in a pleasing, high arc. The cane parted water neatly and vanished. Ducks rushed to the disturbance, heads poked under surface, supposing some sort of food. They speculated noisily. Priest saw the guardsmen ride parallel to the lake, past the girl, toward the bisected length of Route 17. He limped after. Laces on the makeshift sandal popped. He picked up the tread rind. Ducks pecked at the raw club of his foot as Priest lugged it past them. He still held the capsule in his hand. The lower half of the girl's rubber mask was hooped now around her neck. Priest fingered the capsule. Then he tucked it into his breast pocket. It lay outlined, a single nipple. The girl smiled at him. Priest fastened the insect mask across his own expression.

Wild raspberry hedges confounded him. For two hours, for half a mile, they had wallowed in boisterous, prehensile undergrowth. It was useful: it screened them from guard patrols on Route 17. The girl floundered against him. She fell often now; when Priest dragged her up he no longer had patience to be gentle. Her wrist was dislocated, he thought. She didn't complain. It was dusk. To the right, on occasion, he had glimpsed the boxy roof of a house: some suburban avenue there, inaccessible. The raspberry bushes were six feet high. He smelled a sour fragrance. The fruit was immature: pink/white of tweaked human skin. The thorns, though not long, were pesky: he could not draw her easily through them. He was concerned, too, for the fabric of his insect suit. They had walked beyond the Paramus bus terminal. He recognized the rear of a filling station partly bulldozed, a restaurant; north of these, a large half-cylinder building, perhaps a theater or a bowling alley. Priest needed food, shelter for the night. He had to chance coming near the highway.

Priest lifted the girl. She slept at once, as his arms took responsibility for her balance. Crouching, placing the restaurant between them and Route 17, Priest stepped forward. The right ankle was intractable; it allowed him no stealth. The wide dining room was open on three sides. Beige twilight reflected from square, fixed formica tables. Chairs, their wire backs like rug beaters, were tumbled in obeisance, on forehead and knee. Priest set the child down. He peered in. A figure sat, centered, behind one of the tables. His back was to the sunset, he was faceless, but the neck craned impossibly: only a dead man could have held it so for very long. Priest hurdled over the waist-high wall. The man had no mask; insects were strip mining flesh from his face. He loitered in eyeless nonchalance, legs crossed, one hand curled around the stem of a broken wineglass. When death came, there had been something on his knee. He had flicked it off. Thumb and fingers were extended on knee cap; the thing was gone. He reeked.

Two bicycles passed. Priest watched them, mesh eyeholes just above the squat cash register: $7.49 there, archive of some final meal. They rolled tortuously, handlebars jerked by the uneven concrete, south to Route 4. Priest backed inside. The restaurant had no E-diet plumbing. He scanned across two parking lots, toward the half-cylinder building capacious as a hangar. Some public food troughs stood in front of its entrance. Priest climbed out behind the restaurant. She still slept: he worked the child's hands into her insect-suit pockets. Priest went to all fours; he had found himself crawling several times that day. It seemed natural now; it didn't aggravate his ankle. The two parking lots were a hundred feet across. His progress remained secret, suggested above only in delicate shiftings of Canada thistle and cornflower. The weeds were set with Japanese beatles—cheap, burnished-metal jeweling. After twenty minutes he rose on knees cautiously at the first trough's base. E-diet ran in a needle trickling; rust stained the green/gold. He stripped off his insect mask and hood. The hood, inverted, would provide a water bag. Priest stood: it filled very slowly.

He heard a strident squeal, metal turned on metal. Then clanking. E-diet splashed out of the rubber cranium. Two guardsmen were approaching from the south. Priest hobbled

137

anxiously back. The front entrance was too conspicuous. He noticed a wooden structure, built against the hangar's flank, perhaps some storeroom. He hurried there. Priest cursed. The girl was running toward him across the parking lots. He gestured her back/down. The bicycles had come even with the restaurant. Priest could not hesitate. The door was ajar; he squeezed through the splintering crevice.

It was all a hive. Hexagon atop minute hexagon, combs bricked upward. The door, the four walls, were tessellated by drowsing honeybees. Their drone was soporific, low, a snore. Priest stood still. He did not breathe, but his rough entrance had already disturbed them. He heard running outside. Bees dropped onto his bare head and face, lethargic, yet curious. They occupied surfaces of his body, businesslike, soon planning complex scaffolds on him. Priest couldn't suppress his fear. He trembled. And, alert now, the drone changed timbre, rose in pitch; wing after wing increased its frequency. They were alarmed: their great husbandry had been jeopardized. The first one stung him. Priest flailed out, barging against the door. He said no, no, no, and his lips were scabbed with their bodies. Priest shouldered the door; its old wood gave and a latticework comb collapsed entirely there. The hive roared. Hands over eyes, he kicked the door apart. They enveloped his body. As he ran, sightless, toward Route 17, the swarm streamed off his head and shoulders, behind, a comet's tail, some abstract emblem of motion.

The stinging was galvanic, poisonous. Priest wore a skullcap of bees, an elongating cape of bees. His left arm huddled over eyes. Right fist punched savagely at head and throat. Their bodies, crisp nuts, crunched open. His right elbow grazed against the wall, a contact shoe giving direction. He felt the reaction in his heart muscle: a surge of histamines, more dangerous than the stinging itself. He became asthmatic, whooped for air. Bees were in his mouth; tongue scurried to avoid their attack. The wall ended. Priest tottered, then pursued the corner around. A large brass knob winded him. The door was open: he staggered inside, closed it, interdicted the wake of bees behind him. Priest began to kill. He pummeled his body; he ripped hair from beard and scalp, combing through with his fingers. He preferred this pain to the scalding rash on his skin. The bee venom accumulated, neared a fatal concentration. His legs were suddenly wet to the shin. He bellyflopped headlong into the shallow pool, submerged. Bees came off. The pool frothed with them.

The pain ended. Its eerie, quick vanishing scared Priest. Nervous electricity had shorted out. At the jaw, the temples, behind one ear, skin burst open with swelling. Both ankles were the same size now. Hands locked themselves inside his gloves: the fingers spread. Lips, split sausages, were far in front of his mouth. Priest splashed; then he sat outside the rainwater pool. Dim light fell through the holed, high roof: Priest watched cheeks grow under his eyes. The right cheek exploded, spitting blood and lymph. Bees still stung him; there were dozens in the air, but he heard only, did not feel them. Pulse nearly doubled its rate. He was delirious, full of useless, adrenal energy. He swung his arms. A protective, choking mucus closed his throat. Priest raled loudly.

The door opened. Two guardsmen scuttled through. They separated, flanking him, crouched, stun cans out of holsters. Priest recognized the First Monitor's chevrons. He studied their approach idly; he was interested, not yet concerned. His respiration had become rapid and convulsive. He kicked heels in the water. Alternately a flush, a wave of cold goose-flesh, traveled from his forehead downward. Vision closed to slits: his brow ridge gradually protruded. The men unfastened masks. Priest saw the junior guardsman's shark-gash mouth. For a moment, hallucinating, he supposed that this was his own reflection. He tried to shut the mouth, but his tongue, bloated, had wedged between molars. He expectorated dead bees. The First Monitor gestured: Priest stood uncertainly. The junior guardsman bent to collect insect carcasses, evidence. Legally, Priest knew, he had committed murder. While the First Monitor covered Priest with his aerosol can, the junior extracted a death capsule. He forced it into Priest's hand. The fingers would not close. It dropped through.

The junior guardsman chuckled; he acted the fool. His tongue lapped over back wisdom teeth, out of his mouth, a dog panting. He licked high on his own cheekbone, almost to the eye. Priest was fascinated: his brain, delirious, overproductive, tried to rationalize what seemed an illusion. The junior's right eye migrated slowly around the front of his face, the nose turned. Features crowded into profile. The junior held his left arm up at the elbow; he peeled the cuff down, a sleight-of-hand artist's device; Priest was engrossed.

Then the right fist slugged alongside Priest's eye, and Priest heard sssht when the stressed flesh burst again. He fell, legs stiff, rolling over the back edge of his heels. Moon face seemed to deflate: immediately it filled again. Priest saw only from one eye; blood glued the left lids. The junior rammed both knees into Priest's belly, pinned him on the floor. Exhaling, Priest spluttered. Many guardsmen appeared. The many that were the First Monitor stepped closer, aerosol cans fitted each with a medium-distance nozzle. The junior guardsman had pills. Then the junior was made single by a single act: he pinched Priest's lower lip and yanked it down. Priest's body thrilled with a chemical exuberance; he tapped fingers on the wooden flooring, as though impatient. His jaws came open.

The aerosol can fell. It bonked end on end, made a bow tie of blurring motion. It found a slant in the floor, rolled away. The First Monitor scooped with both palms, thumbs outward, perhaps an apology. He sat. He half somersaulted backward, over his kidneys. One knee, the other knee rose; his feet paddled. E-diet spasms folded him relentlessly. Priest glanced up. The junior had just recognized his danger, but he was unwilling to accept it, reluctant even while Priest's fingers felt along his throat. The force of clenching split Priest's swollen gloves. Leisurely, as a lover might, he drew the junior's body down/onto his chest. The guardsman flailed at Priest's ears, but the radius of his punching was constricted. Priest sighed. He pressed the open cheek against his own cheek; passion and release overcame disgust. Priest rolled the guardsman under and mounted him.

141

The capsule lay near his elbow. The man's cheek gash was open, it shivered with breath, a gill. For several seconds the junior's thumbs probed around Priest's eyes, but Priest's arms were much longer. Nails scraped rubber, then flesh from his fingers. Priest's thighs detected a weakening under him. Knees crawled onto the man's arms. Carefully, only left hand against windpipe, Priest picked up the capsule. As if turning a key, he pinched the guardsman's nostrils. Teeth opened with a gush inhale, but they gritted closed when Priest moved his right hand down/away from the nose. Priest considered. He let the man breathe; seemed to consult with him. They stared at each other. Fingers were tapping against his inner arm; Priest did not understand. Then he nodded. He leaned down. His pulpy lips settled over the man's nose. He bit nostrils shut. The mouth opened. Priest stroked throat, Adam's apple until the capsule had gone down. The guardsman's fists pounded the floor. Open hands slapped the floor. Fingertips stroked wood. Then stopped.

The First Monitor had witnessed it. Priest stood over him. He was helpless, body cradled by the spasms, rocking gently. Hands were crossed over his mouth: a stereotype of horror. Priest peeled one hand away, then the other; kneed their palms flat. He fished the child's capsule from his breast pocket. But the guardsman was adamant: his jaws would not open. He seethed air through clenching teeth when Priest shut his nose. Priest found the heavy aerosol can. Without anger, yet insistently, for he was in a hurry now, Priest hammered until the four front teeth had broken away.

PRIEST DREAMED that he was killing Mary. She gave imperturbable birth under him. He rode. His hands flopped on their wrists, stifling pillows. Mary inhaled suffocation as though it were perfumes. Her head unnecked, rolling free of her torso, yo-yoed up/back. It gave splinters. He hurt. Priest knew she was in labor; he hurried the business. Mary's lips reasoned, but he heard no sound. Reluctantly, then, Priest turned her nose off, and it was an old iron faucet: he screwed tight, flakes of bloody rust broke away, her cheeks filled with breath. He shouted, "You're a coward! You're a coward!" The face was two-dimensional, a sheet of mask. He pulled from the right ear, tore it off, tore it off, calendar pages, and the face changed, a smile, a grimace, despair, shame, lust, laughter. But her fecund body was not killed. Enormously, with squeaking release, it was extruded to the waist. A girl. Her face was cauled by strips of rubber.

Priest awoke. Two-by-fours of late-morning sunlight slanted down from a small upper window, half open. He lay in a kind of cellar. Priest smelled humus: its deep rot suggested food. The walls were damp, chalked with lichen clots of efflorescence. He pushed to his knees. He ached;

143

he was shivering. Opposite, brace for the planks of sunlight, a brass handle nosed from the wall. He saw other brass handles, each centering a square of marble; carved inscriptions were above. Priest tried to stand. His tongue used up all oral room: he could swallow without gagging only when he held it down with his forefinger. There was a stubble of festering stings on his neck and forehead, second growth under his beard. He tried to tweeze them out, but fingerpads had swollen against their nails. He was running a temperature. Priest searched across the floor for hood and mask, for his sandal. Then he remembered.

Priest had crushed her chest. He had trampled the child's ribs over her heart. Now, as he remembered, Priest began to squat. His arms dangled over the cement floor; he drummed fists against his shins, rhythms of sullen, autistic reproach from childhood. The guardsmen had intercepted her, administered a capsule before following him into the hangar. Delirious, Priest's mind had inverted actor and victim. He had paused from exhaustion, kicked again, as though packing her into the soil: pauses that made his act seem premeditated and heinous. Then Priest had limped away from Route 17, into retentive, brittle underbrush. He recalled stumbling once, being suspended above the ground in a basket of low brachiate growth, swung there by the whole forest's natural motion. He did not remember climbing into this room; the one window was certainly too high. Yet there were footprints of a biped in the dust: one exact rubber sole, one shapeless, whisking blur.

It was a long room, a rectangle. At the far end, lower

144

steps of a spiral staircase turned upward in wedges. Priest crossed to the wall of handles. He was in a crypt. He read: not one of the dead had been alive a hundred years before. Two brooms leaned, disrespectful, against an island sarcophagus. There was wax on the brass. Priest touched, then flung his hand away. He stumbled back, slapped palms over both ears. For a moment, wavering, he watched the window, watched the staircase. He removed his palms and heard it again: music, whistling. Dumbfounded, Priest held his fingertips together, as if prayerful, until he knew that the sounds were outside his mind. He approached the staircase, swinging from handle to handle. The music was sophisticated. It gave Priest a feeling of madness and thirst. Quietly, on all fours, he climbed the staircase.

The door was ajar. Drafts from the crypt held it open against a weak spring. Priest guessed that this had been a Christian church. The pews were gone: herringbones of wood remained set in the parquet floor. There were a few colored-glass facets on the window leading: at one place a saint's disembodied shins. Columns walked, legs of tall wading birds, along the side aisles. Priest looked up, his elbows on the landing. The arched Gothic ceiling surprised him: he thought of a tent pavilion he had built, four poles and a canvas sheet, blown upward by the wind. Priest pushed the door open. He heard the whistling and there were new dimensions to its tone, echoes. He crept forward, then rose to knees, left hand supporting on the door knob. He glanced toward the half-turret apse. It had no furniture. Soot thumbs reached up, escaping through the broken rose window, ghosts of a conflagration. Priest saw the man.

He was tall. Priest watched him walk toward the apse with big, efficient strides; but there was constraint, too, in the movement. Elbows jutted back; they didn't shift left/right to answer legs' rhythm. His hair was white: it was drifted and crazy. An apron of scalp domed into it. He had an insect suit on, the hood and mask not attached. He was whistling: the sound deepened, thinned, as it rode bowls and rims of the ceiling. Beneath the chancel arch he knelt, sank abruptly below Priest's vision. The whistling unraveled, then stopped. Priest watched for at least ten minutes. He hoped to hear the music again. The man stood: his right forefinger poked forehead, sternum, left pap, right pap. He began loping toward the crypt door. Priest was slow. He scuttled back, stood with one foot on the top stair, waiting for the man to pass. His hand, as it fingered along the brick pointing, scissored a six-foot wooden pole slanted there. Priest hefted it. The whistling began again: Priest could judge the man's progress by it. He was passing then. The door hinges yelped.

The man's height astounded Priest. For an instant, Priest supposed the difference was in him, that his own body had somehow been diminished. Priest had never seen a man that tall. The pole was unwieldy coming out: it clacked on two sides of the door jamb. The man's lips were still puckered; the silent whistle served as a *moue* of surprise. He retreated two steps before Priest thrust. The window pole's iron tip, curled in a beckoning finger, struck, then penetrated his antagonist's chest. It had probed just under the armpit.

Priest's weight, set forward in expectation of a good impact, carried him headlong across the chill parquet floor. He rose to one knee. The man observed him with interest. Priest lifted the window pole. Gently, apologetically, the man trod on its metal tip. Priest wrenched to uproot the clumsy weapon, seemed to crowbar under his opponent's foot. They watched each other. The man shook his head, shrugged. Priest sat awkwardly on his buttocks.

The man settled to his knees; movement was segmented. Priest guessed that he wore a kind of brace. He was very old. His nose had been broken and rebroken: it seemed a flat burrow; nesting animals huddled perhaps under the bridge. Wrinkles graduated his forehead horizontally up to the taut scalp. His eyes were fine, blue; they looked through sparkling layers of rheum. He grasped Priest's arm, tapped there. Priest formed ungainly words. The man was amused. He mouthed fluently.

"You're a mess, my friend. Don't tell me—yes . . . I see the stings. They did a good job on you. I've watched them swarming. They killed a dog last week. Stand up. I can't bend very well." Priest rose. "You're a big bugger, aren't you? Been a while since anyone's head came above my shoulder. I've been shrinking, but seems like the world's been shrinking faster. Can you read my lips?" Priest nodded irritably. "You wanted to kill me." The man smiled. "Yes. But you were too beat up to do it. I was lucky. Don't talk. Come into the light."

He faced Priest toward a window. Deliberately, with eyes close, the old man snipped over Priest's forehead with thumb

147

and fingernail. Priest saw that his skin was weathered, but no yellows undertinged the bronze. Eye whites, too, had not jaundiced. As he concentrated, the upper lip ebbed, tucked atop gums. A fuzzed, oily tartar shod each tooth. His breath stank; the odor troubled Priest. Two large upper incisors were worn and translucent.

"Damn. Never get all these things out. What? Speak slowly. Your mouth is a bloody mush."

"What is this place?"

"A church. You know what that is? Was?" Priest nodded. "Hold still. I'm a priest. A priest, I said." He repeated it, for Priest had frowned: he thought the old man knew his surname. "Last one in the world, I think."

"Why did you whistle? It is against the law."

"You're hearing things, friend. Bees in the ear."

"No."

"Yes. You're hearing things. Believe me. Come in my office; I have something to draw the stings out. And you need medicine for the fever. Hundred two, hundred three at least. I'm surprised you're still alive."

It was a spacious chamber, wonderfully sunlit. Priest, febrile, imagined he was in a child's kaleidoscope, slowly turning with it. One wall had been wholly screened; a roofless overgrown veranda deck extended outside. Insects covered the mesh: June bugs, hundreds of powdered green/white gypsy moths. They tottered under their wings, taxiing aircraft, and early sunlight projected the triangle shapes, exaggerated them, on the whitewashed wall opposite. By agreement they moved in a great clockwise circle; the room

148

appeared to rotate. Five chairs, semicircling, paid attention to the old man's burly desk, a swivel chair behind it: the record of some adjourned meeting. He gestured, left the room. Priest sat. Above, an ingeniously built punkah had been suspended from the ceiling—a yard-square slab of plywood, its energy given by a pedal under the desk. Both walls perpendicular to the screen were bookshelved. Priest saw a table crowded with empty liquor and wine bottles; one decanter of stale, dead-green E-diet. Priest presumed his hunger, did not yet feel it. He was weak. Black granules seasoned the desk top. They pulverized quickly under his thumb. Priest thought, improbably, that these were ashes. The old man returned with a jar of white salve. Rusty oils separated in it, surfaced. He homogenized the salve with a screwdriver shaft, then pulled the swivel chair forward. They sat knee to knee. He anointed Priest's face and neck, his hands. "What is your name?"

"Priest."

"No. Watch my lips. What is your name?"

"My name is Priest. Dominick Priest."

"Ah?" It was almost articulated. "Is that so? A priest in name only. Two of us. Let's see if we can raise your shirt." The old man rolled fabric up/under Priest's armpits. Goose-flesh stippled skin as it bared. "My name is Paul. Xavier Paul." Priest shook his head. The X sound was unfamiliar. "You can read?"

"Yes." The old man wrote it. "X-avier. Xavier."

"Priest, look . . . I'm leaving here; I was on my way

149

when you came. I'm going north to the mountains. You're welcome to stay here until the end."

"No. I am going north. I have a wife and child. I walked three days. Sometimes I have crawled." He locked fingers under his right knee: lifted to show the ankle. "I need food." Priest pointed at the E-diet decanter.

"That's stale." Xavier Paul grinned. "Anyway—can't fool me that easy. You don't drink E-diet."

"I don't? But there is nothing else."

"Your skin is nearly white. Look at that frog's belly." He thumbed up Priest's eyelid. "Your pupils haven't dilated. Tell me the truth."

"Once in three days. That's all. I don't like the stomach pain. I don't like the drug. I have to do things. I have to go home."

"Well—"

"And your skin is white too."

"Well—" Xavier Paul hesitated. "I'll get something for your ankle. I have an old pair of galoshes we could slit. You need a mask and hood. How far are you going?"

"New Loch."

"New Loch?" He laughed: there was sound in the gush of breath. "That's a good thirty miles from here. You'll never make it before the last day."

"I will make it." Priest stood abruptly.

"Sit down. Listen to me. There's no articulation left in that ankle."

"I don't feel pain."

"I didn't say pain—" He gasped. Priest had stamped the

150

right heel. He stamped again. The purple flesh whitened. "Stop it. Are you crazy?"

"I can walk. I have walked from New York City in three days. I don't feel the pain. I don't need my ankle in the grave."

"No. That's true. It's a special time, kind of."

"Let me go now."

"Wait. Sit down. I'm not trying to hold you here." He tapped two yellow pills into his palm. "Take these. They're an antibiotic. Medicine. Worth gold on the black market thirty years ago. I'm not sure if they're good now. They helped me two or three years back. I've kept them sealed in wax."

"No pills."

"You can't swallow? Just let them dissolve on your tongue."

"I don't want pills."

"Why? You can trust me."

"I don't want pills."

"Come. Take them." Priest hit his hand. They skittered across the desk top.

"I see. You're a nasty man, Priest. Just don't press your luck."

"Yes." Priest stood again. "I have been in prison for my anger. What will you do—tell the guardsmen?"

"Relax. What was it—did you think they were death capsules?"

"I have no time for talking. It's late. My wife may be dead now."

"Sit. Please." Priest sat. "It's an idea—I wouldn't mind a traveling companion. How fast can you walk?"

"As fast as an old man can walk."

"I see. Do you still want to kill me?"

"I have killed enough."

Xavier Paul started: he did not question Priest. The lips, he thought, were very hard to read. "An angry man. When it's too late, God sends me an angry man. Twenty-five years ago. I could have used you then." But Priest did not watch the lips. Xavier Paul leaned into his vision. "Don't be a jackass now. See that you're here when I get back."

"Then be quick."

"Be quick. Yes."

"And be alone."

He left. There was a disturbance on the screen. Moths flurried away: the far wall lit up. Priest saw his own silhouette. He reconnoitered the room. Dampness had melded the books: cover dyes leaked into the wood. Priest saw Xavier Paul, a young man, hair dark, brows of smut under the eyes. Shoulders in the photograph were shrugged immensely to his ear lobes; his chest was numbered, 88. Priest limped to the screen. He elbowed it, knocked a chink in the insect shingling. Across the veranda Priest saw a fenced yard grown tumultuous and hazy. Eighteen-inch toadstools squatted, boles muscular as hurdlers' calves, caps canted, rouged at the center. Dandelions and live-forever rooted between veranda planks. But Priest wondered: here and there through a vined trellis he saw dark plots of earth, staked out, cat's-cradled with string. Priest looked down. The screen had come loose. The wainscoting was sugared with white powder. Insects moved in concentric half circles out/away from the powder: crippled, nerveless, spastic; at the wood's rim, dead. Priest bent. He dabbed powder on his thumb tip, then carried it near his mouth. Xavier Paul smacked his wrist. He wiped the thumb on Priest's chest. "Like a child, aren't you? Put everything in your mouth."

"What is it? The bugs are dead."

"Come over here. I thought you were in a hurry."

He made Priest sit. With a honed letter knife, Xavier Paul slashed the neck of one rubber overboot down toward its instep. Priest admired the letter opener. Its handle was ivory, a Maltese cross. Priest stropped his thumb on the blade; it had been whetted beyond a legal tolerance. Xavier Paul watched him. Priest pinched the blade point, held it over his shoulder, hesitated, a request for permission, threw. It severed the spine of a small book; weight gradually pulled the book down/onto its binding. Xavier Paul applauded without sound. Priest was pleased. Then, using his palm as a shoehorn, Xavier Paul gently helped Priest insert his foot into the overboot. He stayed the neck with sections of knotted shoelace. The mask and hood seemed a size too large, but there were no gaps at cheek or throat. Xavier Paul stood. He considered. He thumbed Priest's face at the brow ridge, the long trapezium cheekbones. Priest's eyes stared out of fat slots. Xavier Paul was baffled by their stupidity. He had brought two malacca canes, two empty canvas haversacks. He handed one of each to Priest.

"Follow me," he mouthed. Priest held his arm.

153

"Why do I need the bag?"

"Just be a good boy and follow me."

Priest stood in the crypt again. His breathing was stertorous, oral; his nostrils were shut. Along the side aisle Xavier Paul's gait had appraised him. Step now, check; step now, check. Priest's own cane answered, but joylessly; it was supportive, dull, not a free chorus to his walking. Priest had almost fallen on the spiral staircase. His right foot's new bulk was unfamiliar; it could not judge surfaces. Priest realized that he was sick. Xavier Paul's shoulder ballooned, subsided as he watched it, and the watching had become obligatory. A cymbal rush in his ears accompanied the shoulder's transformation—an -inggg, -inggg, without the initial clash. He wanted the yellow pills now; he was afraid. Xavier Paul walked to the crypt's western end. He waved Priest near. A family tomb had been set into the wall, McCUL-LOCH, two steel doors, handles of twined fruit. One quarter circle had been excised from the dust: recently someone had opened the right door. Xavier Paul wrapped Priest's fingers around the handle. He stood behind him, chest to back, clutched his own hands around, one above, one beneath. A ring on his left hand clacked the steel. Priest was nauseated. The tiny noise echoed unreasonably, gonging, fading, gonging, a klaxon. They drove four legs backward and the door came out. Xavier Paul's lips moved. Priest could not read them. He walked Xavier Paul back toward a single window's light.

"What? I didn't see."

Priest went down. The roar drummed along his spinal

154

cord, clamped his nape. And Xavier Paul was shouting again: "Well? Well? Can you understand me now? Can you, damn it?"

Priest held his ears, but that exacerbated the sound. There was an echo under his muffled palms. He made no sense of it.

Xavier Paul's mouth was wide, ferocious. "Priest," he bellowed. "Priest, I've been in prison too." He clacked teeth together. "For eating." He stepped forward.

Priest crawled away on his elbows. He mouthed, "You spoke. You spoke."

"God damn right I did." Xavier Paul laughed. The sound seemed to pullulate in Priest's head; it spoke crazily of some third person. "God damn right he didddd. God damn right he diddd." Priest glanced at the staircase, at the open window.

"Guardsmen."

"Use your voice. Speak, man. Don't be a coward." Priest flopped onto his stomach. Xavier Paul hauled him upright by the empty haversack. "Priest. You know what I've got in there? Vegetables. Raisins. Figs. Celery. Big fat mushrooms. Salted dog meat." He clapped Priest's shoulder. "And wine. Six bottles of wine. Did you ever drink wine?"

Priest shook his head.

"Three bottles for you. Three bottles for me."

"I—"

"Speak. Speak!" He yelled. "I want company! I want talk!"

"Don't—"

155

"Speak, you coward."

"I'm sick. I'm dizzy."

"Speak! How can men without voices know each other? I'm sick to death of this mincing and miming."

"Give me the pills."

"I'll give you whatever you want. Just speak. Speak. Now."

"The p-ills." At the second word Priest's voice appeared. The "p" remained a suggestion, a pucker, but the plural was hissed.

"Go on. Go on." Priest murmured,

"What if they catch us?" Xavier Paul smiled. "If they catch us, then we'll beat their heads in with our canes. That's what we'll do. We'll beat their stupid heads in."

Priest acted out laughter. Air rasped the membrane of his vocal cords. Priest laughed aloud tentatively, then gleefully. He brayed.

THEY WALKED NORTH on Route 17. Priest was uncomfortable. Xavier Paul had fed him cautiously: three small figs, water for the antibiotic pills. His stomach had clenched nonetheless. It moved as though with knuckles under the skin, a shut fist crushing an insect. He heard trickling: juices overproduced by his enthusiastic, unpracticed glands. For the first time, Priest began to sweat. He found the sensation disconcerting. Saliva troubled his tongue. He spat again and again, for he felt bloated, afraid to swallow. And he had gas: the initial popping bursts had startled him. Priest jumped, looked behind. Xavier Paul laughed. He thought Priest amusing.

Priest talked about Mary. He kept slightly ahead of Xavier Paul, torso turned three-quarters backward, as if to shoulder into head winds. It was useless—his lips were blurred, incoherent under the plastic mask—but Priest didn't yet trust the efficacy of speech. He commented with a free left hand. The words were unelided, set apart for visual reading. He stumbled again and again. Xavier Paul, who had evoked Priest's speech, became silent now, a constraint. He rapped warnings against Priest's knee with his cane. There were

157

numerous guardsmen on Route 17, particularly near the crowded Lesbian Convocation Center at Waldwick. Often Priest yelped words, his voice obstreperous, an unbroken animal. The wine bottles clinked in his haversack. Xavier Paul knew Priest's ankle was destroyed. He would never walk normally again. They were making good progress, however; by three o'clock they had accomplished five of twelve miles to Suffern and the old New York State border.

Xavier Paul learned about Mary, how to hunt her. Priest's wife had many foot shapes, it seemed; they changed with the terrain, with her speed and emotion. Xavier Paul wondered, at first, if this might not be some spirit, tracked in Priest's delirium. But Priest was thorough, impatient: he had much to teach, though Xavier Paul would never cross Mary's spoor. The left small toes were bunched under: you could see their hollowing even through a moccasin's sole. In high grass the business was more challenging, but Mary's legs would move like forceps closed; she was somewhat pigeon-toed. Her breasts were small. Priest did not mean to apologize. Her nipples were fine, large and functional, mahogany-colored, as if iced at their tips with translucent rime. Priest described their sexual games without embarrassment, innocent; yet when he spoke of the woman who had abandoned her child, he became reticent. The story of her death, of her self-abuse with the dildo, was euphemized, made cryptic. Priest had been shocked; he had no charity for her. Xavier Paul guessed that Priest had never known another woman. And Priest mentioned his fatherhood uncertainly. He was not convinced: he had seen neither the thing itself nor its spoor. He smiled. Priest thought he would call his child Xavier. The name had interested him. He asked Xavier Paul to pronounce it. But the name might be difficult for a child. Xavier Paul agreed. Death seemed impertinent then: Xavier Paul did not speak of it.

Near Allendale they watched a mass suicide. Graves had been excavated just inside the highway verge, arced, a lower plate of chunky teeth. Clothing and possessions had been draped on fifteen wooden scaffolds: scarecrows, simulacra of the dead. There were perhaps two dozen spectators. The men stripped; Priest saw that they had been castrated. The leader reviewed them, pausing, as he distributed capsules, at the foot of each grave. Some men embraced. The leader was four feet tall with powerful, grossly bowed legs. He had an awkward stride, as if lifting skis. His own grave faced the half circle. He took position, inclined backward, hands up, buttocks compressed like angry lips. Mosquitoes ate. The men swallowed in unison at the leader's signal, a rehearsed present-arms. They waited, but the capsules killed unevenly. Three men dropped at once, then two: symmetry was ruined. The leader became irritated. He stamped one foot. Three men remained opposite him; one apologized, shrugging. The spectators laughed; they slapped inside their arms. Then three men collapsed. The leader, alone alive, toppled backward prematurely but missed the grave edge. He crawled in on all fours. Priest snorted. Xavier Paul examined the graves. His head was bowed. Some spectators scooped dirt in.

"Exhibitionists," Xavier Paul said. "Poor fools."

"They had no balls," Priest said.

"Yes. You see things simply, don't you?"

The restaurant had not been razed. Anxiously Xavier Paul coaxed Priest toward it. He had dined there often before the Decree. Priest was reluctant to stop, but Xavier Paul had promised him wine. Even thirty years before, the two-story hotel had been ungainly, old. Now a sedate gray lichen had broken out on the wooden façade; ice filaments. The builders had copied a Swiss chalet. In some places Priest saw the hewn log sections, unlit cigar ends; balconies with no access; ogee embellishments under the eaving, around the boarded windows. Behind, a bulldozer had completed one rush at the wall before running down. Jagged force lines radiated in the wood, a cartoon expression of impact. They edged atop the cab, under the upraised blade. Black streaks slithered over brown/yellow in the long kitchen. They had disturbed a colony of chipmunks. The chipmunks exited tumultuously through a wide fireplace, up the chimney. They cheeped as they ran, the sound of newspaper scouring glass.

The dining room preserved surprise. Tables were set, but their chairs had been wrenched to face the doorway. One lay on its back, some waiter's tray between its legs, an exclamation point. Priest and Xavier Paul sensed that their entrance had been acknowledged. Priest set the haversack on a table. There had been tablecloths, but the wood was pulpy now, and the red/white check pattern had become absorbed, a decal. Grubs lived in necklace cells; they inflated slightly, subsided like small lungs. Xavier Paul covered another table with his plastic ground sheet. He served two bottles of Pommard. There were six figs for Priest, six for himself; six button mushrooms each, grown in the crypt; one four-inch thong of dog meat apiece. Priest grinned; the old man's ceremony cheered him. Xavier Paul found two intact wine-glasses. He dusted them with his handkerchief. Red sediment walled the bottles. Xavier Paul drilled their corks out. He gestured to Priest, a man tossing horseshoes. Priest sat. The chair legs developed sudden knees, broke. The chair collapsed. Priest sprawled on the floor. Priest gestured to Xavier Paul, a man tossing horseshoes. Xavier Paul did not sit. They laughed aloud.

Priest was drunk at once. Talking, he bit inflamed parts of his mouth. His voice was hoarse. Xavier Paul did not often understand him. He clutched the wine bottle with both hands, alarmed by Priest's gusto, by the fist that came down when he had no words. Loose grubs were winnowed from the under-table surface, lima beans on the floor. Priest ate wastefully: his throat was constricted and orts of food returned. Priest described Yankee Prison, then the great cable. He began talking disconnectedly of his father. Priest glanced up at Xavier Paul, frowning. He examined the old man's face. Xavier Paul ate primly, pincering, as though he needed to keep his teeth balanced upright. Priest rolled a death capsule up/along his inside pocket lining. He put it on his plate, bisected it with tarnished knife and fork. But the yellow granules distressed him. He threw his plate against the wall. Xavier Paul flinched.

"You have one?" Priest leaned across the table, arms out in a V.

"A pill? Yes."

161

"You will swallow it? Huh?"

"It's strange. In my faith once it was a sin to commit suicide. But now—what does it matter?" He smiled. "At my age it's suicide to live. I could drop dead, here, this minute. I could commit suicide by running, by holding my breath too long. God will forgive my little sin."

"Sin?" Priest screwed a fist into his eye socket: some child suppressing tears. He propped his head on it.

"Sin. Something that is wrong to do." Priest blew at Xavier Paul; he almost spat.

"Something that is wrong to do. You're like all the others; you think Priest is stupid. Stupid is my disguise. No one believed I was smart. So I'm stupid for them." Xavier Paul seemed less tall, sitting. The height was in his legs. "Why do you do it? Die."

"I'm eighty-nine years old. I've kept alive thinking they would need me. When the people revolted. When my God revealed himself." He drank. "But it never happened. I hate these people who hate their own lives. People who are guilty when they breathe with the lungs God gave them, who have no way to expiate their guilt. The world is polluted with despair. They deserve to die. Yet—" he inhaled. "I have been lonely."

"Me. I like to breathe." Priest pounced on the air, mouth ohhed. He choked; laughed at choking.

"I do too. But my lungs seem smaller now. This wine has disappointed me. I looked forward to it. But my tongue is cardboard. There's dust on it. I should have drunk this years ago."

"I like to breathe," Priest repeated. "I don't mind killing the bugs. They're bugs. Who cares about bugs? Who cares for birds and dogs and trees? I want to live with my family."

"Then live." Xavier Paul watched him.

"Yes." Priest smoothed the bottle's flank, as if it had fur and a nap. "And they'll kill me. My wife and my child."

"You could go into the woods. I don't think they would really kill you. They've lost the will. It's just—they've made the world so miserable, death has become a habit with us."

"No. They have strength."

"Don't believe everything you hear. Don't be a child. Don't be gullible. They're effete. Afraid of you."

"I'm not a child. I know them." Priest frowned.

"What do you know? A fool from the country."

"Two of them. Two guardsmen yesterday." He drew his mouth corner back, remembering. "They tried to kill me."

"Bah. You ran away—you only think they would have killed you."

"I didn't run. No." Priest drank. "The bees stung me. I couldn't run. They tried to give me one of the pills. Push it in my mouth. They held me down." Priest pressed the bottle stem against his lips, said, "Ssssh—"

"And? You escaped."

"No. No." Priest smiled. He picked up a table knife. He was wary. "I killed them."

"Good God, man." Xavier Paul closed his fist. A fig's white bowels extruded from the eye of his hand, between thumb and curled forefinger. Then he smiled. "You're lying—dreaming."

163

"I am not." Priest was insulted. "I won't tell you things if you don't believe me."

"No. On second thought—I do. I believe you. It was a shock to hear it; that's all." Xavier Paul looked away, at the floor. Some of the chipmunks had returned. Xavier Paul preferred to address them. "He killed two men yesterday. And we talk about bugs."

"They killed the little girl. Did I say that? I didn't want to kill them." A fork pierced through the ground sheet, through the pulpy sheath of wood rot. It stood upright. The handle sang when Priest's fingers released it. "They made me angry. They killed the little girl—but I didn't know it then. No. I only knew it after." Priest held his lower lip. "It was the bees. They stung me. But you said it too. You said we'll bash their heads in with our canes."

"I—that was just a manner of speaking."

"Whack. Whack. Whack. The second one didn't want to eat his pill." Priest dramatized. He waited for Xavier Paul's reaction sullenly. "So I broke his teeth in."

Xavier Paul drank half a glass of wine. Said nothing.

"Was that a sin?"

"Mmm?"

"I think you're afraid of me, old man."

"Yes. Not that you might kill me, Priest." But that was a rationalization, Xavier Paul thought. Death under Priest's hands had a special horror. He repeated, "Not that you might kill me. I'm afraid of something in your eyes. Or—something that isn't in your eyes." He laughed. His voice became shrill. "Don't worry about it. Why worry if I'm afraid?"

164

"Oh." Xavier Paul had disappointed Priest. "It's funny. I was afraid of you before, back there. I thought you were a ghost; I didn't think you were real."

"Maybe we should go now."

"You don't answer me. Was it a sin? Did I make a sin?"

"Ah—" Xavier Paul had become careful. "In another time, in my time, I think they would have said self-defense."

"There is no self-defense. We are told that. It is rule number twelve. Priest read it."

"Rule number eleven. They tell you wrong, Priest."

"Yes. Is that so?"

"It is. Damn—I absolve you of the guilt. That is—if you feel any guilt, which I doubt." Xavier Paul performed the sign of the cross with his right hand. "Were you a Christian? Were your mother and father?"

"I don't think so. How do I know? No one ever told me anything."

"Let's see—you were ten at the Decree. It's possible you were baptized."

"What is that?"

"A priest puts water on your head." Priest fingered his temples. "He grants you freedom from sin and a promise of eternal life." Priest nodded: he thought the old man was crazy. "Jesus Christ—have you ever heard of him?"

"The name. Yes. Who is Jesus Christ?"

"Is? Was." Xavier Paul moistened his lips. "Is. Jesus Christ is the Son of God. Two thousand years ago he was crucified on a cross. He died to take men's sins away."

"What was that word? Crucified?"

Xavier Paul sighed. He opened his arms, seemed to measure a segment of the air. "They hung him on a wooden cross. Nailed him to it through his hands and feet. Until he died."

Priest considered this. "What god? What god was his father?"

"The God who rules all things. What other God?"

"Oh." Priest shrugged. "That god."

"Jesus Christ gave his flesh and blood for us." Xavier Paul became eager. "That's why they closed our churches. They said it was cannibalism. And anyway, we couldn't sacrifice . . . there was no more bread, no more wine. E-diet is not Christ's blood. It has no life in it."

"You believe this?"

"Yes."

"Mmm. Is there more wine?"

"Not for now. Later. Tonight perhaps." Xavier Paul licked ooze of the broken fig from his palm. "It's been a long time. I haven't talked about Christ in a long time."

"I've seen your crosses. In a cave near my house. Mary and I used to play there. It was where the Christians stayed in the war."

"Where?"

"In the cave."

"No." Xavier Paul rapped the table excitedly. "Where is the cave?"

"Oh. Behind a mountain called Bull's Hump. West of New Loch. It's high on a cliff. But the path broke. I—we couldn't go there any more. We found bones." Priest licked the bottle's snout. Xavier Paul clutched fingers in his beard, hung his arm on them.

"I wasn't there. I was in the battle of the Palisades." He worked up one sleeve: there was an empty pod, a crater above the wrist. Notches had been sawed from the radial bone. The flesh appeared silvery. "I was a colonel in the Christian Legion. But we weren't all Christians. It was just a name."

"Yes?" Priest had lost interest. "You going to eat that fig?"

"Yes. It's my fig." Xavier Paul took it. "I lived off the land two years before I heard about the amnesty. Near Lake Shanatati. That's where I'm going now. It's on the other side of the old Thruway. I'm going to eat Jesus Christ's flesh and blood there. A last time before the end." Priest glanced at him.

"Do you eat this flesh and blood? In your mouth?"

"Yes. I make the mass." Xavier Paul winked. "You don't live to eighty-nine just eating the E-diet."

"Mass. Mass." Priest liked the word. "Do all Christians eat?"

"Yes. They did once. I haven't seen another Christian in twenty years. I haven't baptized a child into the faith since—" He thought. "But I haven't looked for them. I've been slack. Tired—tired of the whole thing. I've spent twenty years planning meals. Hiding food like a squirrel. Wolfing things down in the dark. They caught me at it twice. Once, ten years ago, I found a supermarket storeroom. Some of the cans were—"

"Let me see it."

"What?"

"Christ's flesh and blood. Is it in the sack?"

"Priest. You make me sick." Xavier Paul grimaced, shook his head. "Listen: it's just a symbol. We use bread and wine, wafers and wine, to represent the flesh and the blood. Christ died two thousand years ago. I explained that."

"You won't share it with Priest. You want it all for yourself."

"For God's sake. Look—I just said. It's wine like the wine you've been drinking. But it doesn't become the blood of Christ until you're baptized into eternal life."

"Yes?" Priest was suspicious. "Eternal life. What does that mean? The guardsmen can't kill you?"

"I'm sorry. This is my fault. I forgot just how abysmally stupid you are. There was a time when these things had meaning for all people." Xavier Paul ate the fig quickly. "Eternal life isn't this life. You die. All men die. But if you believe in Jesus Christ—then you have another life after this. With God."

"Where?"

"With God."

"Where? Where is God?" Priest smirked.

"In a better place than this. You can be sure of that."

"You eat the flesh and the blood there?"

"I guess. We're getting nowhere. Let's go."

"Baptize me." Xavier Paul laughed. "Why are you laughing?"

"Baptize you? This is no joke, no game. It's not like putting on a new shirt. You have to believe—"

"I believe."

"Like hell you do."

"I believe."

"You don't even know what I'm talking about." Xavier Paul stood. Priest pushed the table. Xavier Paul tottered back, sat again.

"You old horse. You'll eat it all yourself."

"Calm down. You're drunk, Priest. You're not used to the wine. We're friends. I'm not trying to cheat you." Xavier Paul placed his palms on the table. He soothed the wood. "Maybe I will baptize you. I have to tell you more about it. We have time."

"Does it taste good?"

"Yes, but it's just bread and wine; I told you that. When you believe in Christ it feels good. In here." He touched a place on his sternum.

"Ah—" Priest stood. He was afraid.

"What is it? What's the matter?"

Priest had hiccuped. He was startled by the reflexive plucking. He had not hiccuped in thirty years. His eyes opened. Priest had heard of heart attacks. He thought this was some eccentric and hazardous systole beat. Hands palpated over his thorax. He stumbled, more obviously drunk now that he required balance. It happened again. Xavier Paul began to laugh.

"What? What-up?"

"Priest, you should see your face."

169

"My heart—"

"Heart? It's hiccups, you jackass. You must have had them as a child. It won't kill you. I get them all the time."

"Hic-ups?"

"You're not used to eating. Ssssh—close your mouth. We can't go outside if you make that noise." But Priest had become interested: the peevish sound amused him. He lowered his jaw, exaggerated it, laughed.

And saw his laughing. Priest cringed down. A full-length mirror walled one thigh of the kitchen doorway. Priest parried defense with the wine bottle in his hand: another bottle answered exactly. He was afraid, paranoid. His arm muscles rolled, as though testing the bonds of this automatic repetition. Priest stepped nearer. The mirror was old, smoky. Flakes, less reflective, metaled its surface, droplets of mercury pressed flat between glass slides. Nacre rainbows edged them. He buffed in front of his face with one hand; the mist, he thought, was imitated from the room's air. The mirror hand wiped, but not mimicking now, made to mimic. He hiccuped. Priest lifted the wine bottle. Yet he had superstitions of identity. The bottle did not strike. Xavier Paul stood behind him. He was taller. Counterfeiting play, Priest rammed his forearm across the old man's shoulders. Xavier Paul exhaled; his back seized up. He clutched palms on hips, legs apart. His stomach distended, as though he were defecating. Priest was alone inside the mirror.

"Damn. Don't do that, you fool." Xavier Paul hissed breath, wary of a quick inhale. "You hurt my back." He brought feet together, straightened, a chain losing slack link by link. "Jesus Christ, the pain."

"Jesus Christ," Priest repeated. "Delicious. Delicious." He hiccuped. He smiled. His teeth worked, chewing in the mirror.

Priest stood still. The mountains were dead. Their scalps appeared gray, seborrheic. The trees were leafless. Xavier Paul imagined stripped boys, their bulk and vanity gone, yet not shy. Each wore an ivory knee sock. It was seven o'clock. The sun had set unevenly: shadowed here, but still bright on the valley's northeastern crest. Flocculent vapor issued from the frontal lobe of Conklin Mountain, from the shoulder of Squirrel Swamp Mountain. Xavier Paul and Priest waited in the highway bed. Route 17 curved right to the Thruway exit at Suffern. An unorganized herd of deer loitered near Torne Brook. They were emaciated. Priest said, pointing,

"Smoke?"

"No." Xavier Paul stubbed the pavement. Fissures there were calked with a brown/black bead of caterpillar bodies. "Gypsy moths."

Priest walked ahead. He unsnapped his mask. The vapor bursts, he saw, were faceted, made of planes that caught or dulled the twilight. As they flocked, the moths seemed to blink, shiver, ashes blown from a cold paper fire. Deer walked somnolently at all levels to the arid crag summit of Conklin Mountain. Trunks had been neatly shucked. Deer stood on hind legs nuzzling the highest cuticles of bark. Torne Brook was red/brown. Its banks were eroded, as

171

though mazy tree roots had been drawn out of the soil. Priest turned. He stared at the great factory.

"The deer are starving. I've never seen so many. There were a lot last winter. The bodies stank when it thawed."

"Yes. And it's summer. Or an endless winter just beginning." Priest gestured to the Thruway. He was sober now; his head ached.

"Are you going that way?"

"It doesn't look very pleasant, does it?" Xavier Paul rolled a ball of the blurred caterpillars. Kneaded it with his sole. "Might as well die with the land. Yes. I'll go north to Route 210, then east. I'll leave you there."

"It will be dark soon. I don't like sleeping with these things."

"We can go in there." Priest looked.

It seemed a bare acropolis, thirty acres square. Rectangular dolmens studded the mesa roof, pedestals perhaps for some pantheon no longer honored. Deer inhabited the wide center forum, dwarfish there, frustrated by outcroppings and crevices that grew no food. A soil ramp had been bulldozed up/against its rear wall, over bumpers of a railroad spur, but the roof had not been landscaped. A Guards flag drooped, unable to catch wind, holed in six places. To Priest's left the sign asserted: FORD. In the distance a leviathan water tank had fallen into its tripod tower, an egg grabbed by some spindly closing lap. One equatorial split opened it. But from Route 17 the building appeared intact. Windows were unbroken. Priest thought the walls had been painted.

"What was in there?"

172

"An automobile assembly plant. It's a museum now. I don't see anyone, do you?"

"No." Priest thought. "Ford. Yes, I remember."

"Let's try it. Are you game, my friend?" Priest nodded. "And, for God's sake, watch your big mouth."

"I know. I know. It was the wine before."

Deer had groomed the vegetation. Dandelion stems were cropped to the soil line, pinched at their ends, straws sucked flat. At first Priest thought they had stepped on broad flagstones. But the stones resounded, gave: car roofs. Fill had been patiently shoveled over/between hundreds of automobiles never driven. Priest stamped on a red blister: rabbits puffed, smoke exhaust, from holes around the buried car. Its interior was a warren. They disturbed shrews, chipmunks, a woodchuck. Priest laughed, stamping, stamping. Xavier Paul hushed him; he was tired and cranky; Priest's enthusiasm had become tedious.

The door opened. For twenty yards they were purblind, groping over opposite walls of a narrow foyer. Then skylights illuminated the main assembly room. Its twenty-foot-high roof was hung with mobiles, rotating gently on their chains; chassis and car segments dangled down, steps in a process, to the ingenious assembly line. It was the moment, preserved after thirty years, when ecology commandos had blown up the Kings Point generator. Priest was thrilled. He hurried along the line, in reverse, one hand out, feeling and seeing, as the automobiles were picked down to their carcasses. Several partitions had been arranged around the spacious front area, once a sales office; the museum. Xavier Paul

173

reconnoitered thoroughly; they were alone. He sat on the floor to wait for Priest.

"So many cars. I didn't think there were so many cars. And all those outside." Priest hobbled back. He was disheartened. "What's wrong with you?" Priest thought Xavier Paul had fallen.

"I'm all right. Tired." Xavier Paul extended a hand. "Gently now, you big baboon. You've wrenched my back once already." Priest helped him up.

"My father worked on cars. I told you that."

"No. You didn't."

"I helped him. I was good with my hands. This makes me remember. I liked to drive fast on the roads. But no one will drive again, I guess."

"No."

"In this place of eternal life . . . Are there cars?"

"I don't think it's one of God's priorities."

"What does that mean?"

"No cars."

"Oh—" Priest stepped around a wall. The office area had been stripped of its furniture, its dividers. A single long room now, it ran the building's full width at the front. "What is this?"

"The museum." Priest pointed. "That? That's an Eisenhower light tank. They used tanks in the war. Terrible things. If we'd had just a few tanks when Hauser turned Gregory's right flank—" He shrugged. "Well, we all ran short of fuel in the end."

"They shot bullets with that? Jesus Christ, it's big." Xavier Paul grimaced.

"It's a cannon, Jesus Christ. That's what put me out of action. A cannon. August 16, 2006. Foggy day it was. I don't remember the night." Xavier Paul massaged his forearm.

Priest knelt. He examined the hard treads, one by one, muttering: said a giant's rosary. He stood in front to imagine the tank's crushing impetus. It scared him pleasantly. He hammered at the steel breastbone with his fist. The machine gun did not swivel in its slit. Other weapons were displayed on a platform along the center aisle: a howitzer, a bazooka, a flame thrower. Two manikins modeled standard combat equipment. Priest assaulted one from behind, wrist under chin, presumed knife hacking down. The head came off. Priest giggled. He replaced it backward.

"No one will sneak up on him again. He can see his own ass now. What's that thing?"

"Helicopter gunship. It could fly up or down." Xavier Paul raised, lowered his palm. "We had six of them, but only two experienced pilots—"

"Look at this."

Priest was distracted again. He limped ahead, jerking Xavier Paul after. In one corner a thirty-foot-square panorama of Manhattan Island stretched to the wall horizon. Gauze represented pollution: it was tinted black/gray. A few penthouses and spires had been inserted through. The rivers were a sluggish gumbo, stewed with fat chunks of sewage. Manikins superintended the display. They wore masks, oxygen tanks: MAN CIRCA 1990.

175

"That's the bridge I crossed." He traced a thread cable with his forefinger.

"Amazing. You must have ice water in your veins."

"Priest was scared a little." He grinned. "Back then, was it really like this?"

"No. Exaggerated. They exaggerated everything. And now we wear masks anyhow."

"Look. Guns." It was a case of pistols. "You think they still work?"

"Perhaps. They seem well enough kept."

"I want one."

"What for?" Priest clubbed down with both elbows. The pane did not break: it dropped neatly out of the wooden frame. Priest lifted the glass, slanting it on one edge. He withdrew a blocky, square .45 pistol. There were three clips of ammunition.

"It's heavy. My father had a gun, but not like this. Smaller, I think. Look. There's grease on it."

"I see."

"Can you load it?"

"Probably."

"Go ahead. Load it."

"You must think I'm crazy." Xavier Paul walked away. "You're dangerous enough as it is."

"This thing goes in the handle, doesn't it? Like so."

"Damn it, Priest. Be careful."

"Well. You do it then."

"Why?"

"Because." Priest was cunning. "I want to die this way.

176

Not with pills. That's a woman's way to die. What is this thing for?"

"The safety lock. Here, give me that." Xavier Paul hesitated, then injected the clip. "I'm doing a foolish thing."

Priest put the extra clips into his thigh pouch. He took off his gloves, rubbed palms together. "Let me hold it. Let me."

"Damn kid. Just don't take the safety off." He gave Priest the .45. "Watch where you point it."

"Bah! Bah, you're dead." Priest aimed at one of the manikins. "Bah! He's dead. Dead. Right in the eye." He hefted the pistol; he liked its weight. "Wonder if this really works?"

"Just wonder. Just keep wondering. God, you make me nervous."

"Yes? I've been nervous all my life. Now let someone else be nervous."

"Put it away, please."

"Hey, let's take a ride."

"Slow down for one minute, will you? We need sleep and food."

"Get in. Get in."

The convertible was on a low dais: SUNDAY DRIVERS, CIRCA 1990. Two manikins—a male and a female—waited in the front seat. They wore goggles, complex inhalers. A papier-mâché spaniel stood on four legs behind them, also goggled, masked. Priest shook the steering wheel. He opened a rear door: knelt in, sat. He laughed. He tapped the driver's shoulder. Xavier Paul shook his head. Priest leaned forward, tongue out, a third lip. He cupped left palm under the manikin's breast. He panted. Xavier Paul was not entertained. Then Priest reclined, heels up/on the front seat back. He patted the dog.

"Get in."

"Aren't you tired?"

"I'm tired. I'm tired. That's why I'm in here. Seat's comfortable." He slapped the fabric. "Soft. Get in. Don't be an old crotch." Xavier Paul opened the other door. He sat, the dog between them. It was nearly dark then: Priest could distinguish only a side lock of Xavier Paul's white hair, and a bent wire, his profile, down from it. "Nice."

"Yes. Nice. Never enough leg room. I had a Ford. I could have driven it with my knees."

"There's no gas around, huh? You don't think—maybe they have gas in here someplace."

"I wouldn't think so. What does it matter?"

"We could make time in a car." He hit the door. "I'd like that."

"Yes. . . . Of course the roads are useless." Xavier Paul hawked saliva. "The tires are flat. No oil in the engine. But we could take turns pushing."

"Oh?" Priest craned over the door's sill. "The tires are flat? I didn't see . . ." He paused. "Well, but we did good today. Tomorrow I'll be home maybe. Don't you think?" Xavier Paul had dozed. Priest pushed his arm.

"Ah . . . What?"

"You think I'll be home tomorrow?"

"Twenty miles yet. No. Day after that." Xavier Paul

rubbed his face. "I didn't think you'd get this far. How's the ankle?"

"It hurts." Priest lifted the right foot. He untied cords of his overshoe. "In the toes. Along my shin. It goes thump-thump."

"Good. At least it's alive. My back's not so hot. I wonder about tomorrow morning. I've been laid up for weeks at a time with it." Abruptly Priest leaned forward. He pushed fingers under the female's inhaler strap, caressed nylon hair. He sat back heavily.

"She doesn't know I'm coming. I wish she knew." He worked the overboot off. "Maybe she's taken the pill by now. It's no good up there. All her friends are in the lesbian commune. They do what the guardsmen say. And Ogilvy . . ."

"Ogilvy?" Xavier Paul yawned.

"He—once he . . ." Priest contracted Xavier Paul's yawn.

"Well, it's in God's hands."

"I want to see her again." Priest spoke harshly, as though Xavier Paul had some decisive influence, could be persuaded. "I want to see her again."

"I know you do."

"It can't be . . ." He shook the dog. "After all that. After the bridge and the bees. The pain. The guardsmen. It can't be she's dead."

"They're dead."

"What do you mean?" Priest groped at Xavier Paul's shoulder. "What d'you mean, they're dead?"

"Nothing. I mean we can't know. This world is stupid and tiresome."

"She's dead." Priest gasped. "I just got a picture in my head."

"You can't know."

"I just got a picture. I saw it. I should never have killed them."

"What was that?" Xavier Paul sat rigid.

"She was dead, and the child—"

"Ssssh—"

The main door had been opened: a draft verified the faint sound of hinges. Xavier Paul and Priest became still, heads inclined to imitate the dummy heads. Light then: a blue glow shone as if through watered milk. Two men came in. One held a chemical Phosphere. By its weak light they saw green shoulders. The guardsmen chatted with their fingers; masks had been unsnapped. Priest tugged up the flap of his thigh pouch. Xavier Paul thought this was not a regular patrol: the guardsmen dawdled; museum exhibits intrigued them. Priest had the .45 out. Xavier Paul saw its square muzzle near the spaniel's right forefoot. One guardsman hesitated in front of the broken gun case. He held the Phosphere over a notepad for several minutes while he wrote. Priest, Xavier Paul guessed, had begun to smile, to sneer perhaps; the compact profile bracket of his mouth had opened. The guardsmen walked toward them; they were not alert. One rocked the convertible aimlessly, pumping down with two hands on its right fender. The female dummy, unbalanced by Priest's caress, fell forward, temple against the dashboard. One guardsman jumped aside, stun can drawn. The other shoved him between the shoulder blades. Xavier Paul and Priest heard hissing: a muted, derisive laughter.

Priest brought the .45 up. Xavier Paul closed thumb and forefinger over his wrist. Priest was astonished by the grip. His hand almost gave up the gun butt. He felt his own pulse thud in Xavier Paul's thumb pad. They wrestled with impassive faces, arms below the front seat back. One guardsman righted the female manikin gallantly. He put lips on the unknuckled, white mitten of her hand. Xavier Paul thought he was drugged. For a moment the guardsman stared at Priest: the insect suit seemed incongruous. But it was dark, and his mistake with the dummy had demoralized judgment. He clicked the door button in and out. His partner swung the Phosphere on its chain like a censer above the panorama of New York City. He turned. He began walking toward the exit.

Priest was exasperated. He cursed when the main door shut, though not audibly. Xavier Paul unwound his grip. He heard small thunder outside as the guardsmen buckled sunken car roofs. Priest hit the dummies. He broke the dog in half: it tore, a loaf of stale bread, across his chest. He was angered by Xavier Paul's interference: infuriated, too, by his successful strength. The old man ignored him. The stress had referred pain to his spine. He panted, lungs taxed by the necessity of shallow breathing. Priest opened the right rear door. He stood, his back to Xavier Paul. The .45 pointed, pointed: a general accusation.

"I couldn't let you do it," Xavier Paul grunted. "It wasn't necessary."

"No? What if he saw me? Huh? He had a stun can."

"They were drugged. It was dark."

"You're a coward. You're like the rest of them." He mimicked the hoarse, profound voice. "We'll bash their heads in with our canes. Oh, yes—know what you are? A fake, that's what you are. A ballsless, yellowbelly fake. I thought you had guts. Good, I said; this is a man. That's what I thought. Stupid Priest. Stupid I am."

"I'm going to die soon, my friend." Xavier Paul crossed the rear seat carefully, pushed himself upright. "I need to make peace with my God. I'm not a free agent like you. My hands aren't clean. In eighty-nine years there's time enough for sin. Time enough. Try to understand that. You see things in flashes and explosions. You have no gentleness." He touched Priest's shoulder. His fingers were pried away. "I don't blame you. I don't. Anyway, thanks—you could have fought my hand off. But you didn't."

"No. I couldn't. You were pushing down. You're heavier than I am, you big ox." Priest turned. He aimed the .45 at Xavier Paul's breast. "I could have shot them, then you. First them, then you."

"So shoot. Now."

"Maybe I will."

"Wait. I have an idea." Xavier Paul stuck his forefinger tip in the pistol's barrel. "Let's eat first. Let's have some wine. I'd prefer to be shot on a full stomach."

"Eat your own guts, funny man. Hey—wait a minute."

182

Xavier Paul glanced at the floor. Priest was staring down. "Hey."

"What is it?"

"Hey." Priest dropped the .45. He was confused by surprise. Hands trussed his abdomen, then lower, his groin. "Hey. Hey. Hey."

"What is it? Tell me."

Priest bowed. Thumbtips dug under his tough, ligamented waistband. With the noise of breaking suction, Priest's insect-suit pants came down. Xavier Paul saw his nude groin and thighs. The pubic-hair smoke billowed over his genitals, as though they smoldered. Priest turned his legs out, rose on tiptoes. He began to urinate, spurting. He slung his member in both hands awkwardly, an amateur at this, and lashed the stream upward.

"You old bastard. I'm pissing. I'm pissing again. Hey. Look at that."

Urine dashed Xavier Paul's chin and throat: it was pleasant, sweet. Wine, hardly digested. Priest whooped, his head back, a naughty gargoyle gutter. Then the old man stripped. For a few seconds they dueled, rooting with curses, laughing, in the dead factory. Body-warm urine ran off their waterproof chests.

It had begun to drizzle. Thunder ground overhead. The factory roof collated rain, herded it along crevice and watershed, guessing a route of subtle gravities, down. Pools swelled, canal locks filling, until they brimmed an obstacle. Here and there cascades sluiced through the roof. The windshield seemed to crack with spatters. From twenty feet up, a big wallet of rain burst noisily over the vinyl car roof. Priest and Xavier Paul were in a large sedan. They had finished one bottle of wine each. Xavier Paul slept full length on the rear seat, naked triangle shins out the window. It rained on his feet. He snored marvelously.

Priest could not sleep. Hurrying metabolism had wasted the wine stupor. He heard his own voice: it blurted answers to the roof rain. His throat was sore. Priest had used it inexpertly. His body twitched in a reprise of the day's emergencies. Legs ran, sets of two steps, before he could stop them. The swelling had ebbed: he could recognize metatarsal bones along the instep. In his abdomen—weightless moment at the crest of a fall—he was startled and restartled, adrenal responses but without stimuli. He made fists that hurt his fingers. And he was afraid.

The picture of Mary dead had returned twice. Unreasonably Priest supposed a poleaxing blow. Mary's limbs spastic at the instant of collapse, her sudden gracelessness more dreadful than death. Priest was suspicious of this vision. He thought it a secret wish. He tried to assemble Mary's face, but the usual, sure devices were inefficient. He concentrated on the form of her nose and ears, simple geometry: the nose plain, wedge-tipped, a specific blush on the lip below, and, during cold days, clear drops of water there, her warmth condensed; ears shark-finned back to a point, morning-glory leaves that cut through her persistent brown hair. But now these images were useless; and for the child he had no images at all. Priest was superstitious. He felt strong desire for Mary, not sensual: her stomach, her breasts were an ostrich hiding place for his body. He burrowed eyes in the plastic seat back. Legs walked again. He sweated; he stank of anxiety. He said that he loved her, half a dialogue, imagining Mary present, but it was unnatural. He had never spoken to her aloud. He groaned. Priest loathed Mary for his great dependence. The snoring maddened him. Priest hurled his sodden shirt. "Shut up!"

"Uh? What?"

"Shut up. Your stupid snoring. I can't stand it."

"Where is this? Oh." Priest heard movement. "What did you say?"

"I said, your damn, stupid snoring—I can't stand it."

"Yes?" Xavier Paul yawned, smacked his lips. "Sorry about that. Mmm. I was fined for snoring once a week, back then, when I was living with people. They put gags in my mouth, made me sleep standing up. I've never heard it myself, though. Couldn't wake up quick enough."

"It stinks. Sounds like you're puking to death. I wanted to strangle you."

"That bad? Say . . . started to rain." Xavier Paul drew his shins in. "What time is it?"

"Who knows? Midnight? One o'clock?"

"Is that all? Thought it was near dawn. At my age you don't need much sleep. Did I wake you up?"

"I haven't slept yet. I haven't had a minute's sleep. I can't."

"Not even with the wine? The wine puts me out like a light."

185

"No." Priest steered the car negligently with one hand. He couldn't see Xavier Paul; it made him nervous. "My body is running. I've been going for so many days now. I can't stop. I want to move."

"You need sleep, though. Ahhhh." Xavier Paul sat up. "Feel like a broken-backed cat. My spine is in pieces."

"I'm worried." Priest said it angrily. "I think my wife is dead."

"Yes. There isn't much time left." Xavier Paul groped in his haversack. He found a curved pipe, packed it. "My last half pound of tobacco. After thirty years I timed it pretty well. And twelve matches." He lit the pipe. Priest saw him: saw his selfish absorption.

"You don't care," he snarled. "You're going to die. You don't love anyone. You've been alone too long."

"Wait." Xavier Paul tamped the pipe with his little finger, holding the lit match pinched over it. "I do care. Mmm. I've prayed for you and—Mary? Mary's her name, isn't it? We're all going to die, Priest. She won't have pain. You'll meet her again in a better life."

"You say that. You keep saying that."

"I believe it."

"But you haven't baptized me. And who will baptize Mary?"

"Baptize? Oh, you remember that. Well . . . God appreciates the circumstances—"

"I don't believe any of this."

"Take my word for it." The bowl glowed.

186

"Why should I? Why is this other life so wonderful? Are there bodies in this other life? Are there things to do?"

"Things to do?" Xavier Paul puffed. "Our souls grow up, Priest. We see things differently. You don't want the things of your childhood now, do you?"

"Yes."

"Yes?"

"I want to be a child again."

"Well . . . perhaps you do."

"Perhaps I do. Perhaps I do. You make me sick. You sit there making that ugly smoke. What do you care? Huh?"

"You're in a foul mood."

"Yes. Yes, I am."

"I understand. You're upset." Xavier Paul changed the subject. "Look. Tell me more about Mary."

"You don't want to hear."

"I do. I do."

"But that just makes it worse. Talking about her. Why should I drive myself crazy?"

"You'll think anyway. Talk about her. Then she'll become part of me, too." The bowl seemed to wink. "It'll give her a sort of life here." This intrigued Priest. He thought for a moment.

"Mary is a woman." Priest hesitated. He could not express her further. He rolled the car window down. "You know what I mean?"

"Yes. Go on."

"Well. What do you want me to say?"

"I don't know. If I did, then I wouldn't have to ask."

187

Xavier Paul ticked a thumbnail on the pipestem. "Why do you love her?"

"Why?" It seemed a pointless question. "She loves me. I love her."

"Is that why you love her? Because she loves you?"

"Look—" Priest was annoyed. He extended his palm, cupped it for the rain, licked. "This is a waste of time. I don't speak good. I show how I feel by doing things."

"By hitting people or kissing them? Yes." Xavier Paul coughed circumspectly, braced his back. "But you don't need poetry. You can talk about her. Simple words are enough."

"Mary loves me. She doesn't have to say it. She doesn't look at me the way those other women do. As if being a man was a stupid, ugly thing. Lesbians that make sex with their mouths. I saw it once. It was disgusting. I wanted to vomit."

"You're a prude, Priest. Bless your heart." Xavier Paul laughed. "A real Mrs. Grundy, what they used to call a bluenose. The beast is a prude."

"Beast?" Xavier Paul heard Priest turn toward the back seat. "What do you mean by that? Beast?"

"Keep your rubber pants on. Take it easy." Priest saw upper lip, part of Xavier Paul's nose, above the pipe bowl. "Men are beasts. That's what they should be. You're a man. Right?"

"That's not the way you said it."

"So sensitive."

"You make fun of me."

"No. No, I'm not. This interests me, that's all. You can kill. You're a bit superstitious about it, perhaps, but not

188

guilty. Yet a bunch of harmless lesbians offends you. A few hours ago, Priest—you would have murdered two guardsmen, yet everything has to be proper."

"I say what I feel." Priest was uncertain: he sensed cruelty in Xavier Paul's tone. "Did you ever have a wife?"

"No. I was old-fashioned. I didn't think priests of God should marry."

"Did you ever make love to a woman?"

"Sorry, Priest." Xavier Paul tapped his pipe on the windowsill. "You're not my confessor."

"Confessor? What is that?"

"Before a Christian can eat the bread and the wine, he confesses. Tells his sins to a priest. Asks forgiveness. The priest is his confessor."

"The bread and the wine . . ." Priest was hungry again. "When you eat, who is your confessor then?"

"I have none, obviously."

"Then I am your confessor."

"Ah?" Xavier Paul blew into the pipestem. "No. I don't think so, my friend."

"Why not? Because I am a beast? When you die—who will you confess to? You will eat the flesh and blood then."

"To myself, of course. The Lord God has good ears." Xavier Paul yawned. "You forget, I have been both sheep and shepherd for twenty years."

"Too much of yourself." Priest spat; Xavier Paul laughed.

"Don't you like me, Priest?"

"I don't trust you. I don't trust anybody. The world is

189

full of stinking corpses. I don't like the dark. I want to see where you are."

"I'm not going to attack you."

"You might rape me."

"That's not particularly funny."

"I don't think you ever had a woman. I think you're queer."

"That will be enough."

"I think you—"

"Shut up, Priest."

It was a command. Spare, effective; just stated. A light blow struck by some terrific, inertial weight. Priest was apprehensive. Spite opened his mouth, but he was awed and did not answer. He could not trade strengths: a shriek alone would have matched that rich assurance. Secondary rain from the roof slackened. Priest sat behind the steering wheel, forearms wrapped in a breast stroke around it. He was furious: thwarted, impressed. Xavier Paul lifted his legs up/onto the front seat back. Priest pumped the accelerator. He broke the gearshift. He heard the old man's stomach gush and whirr. They did not speak for half an hour. Xavier Paul lit the pipe again, smoked, tapped it out. Reluctantly Priest spoke first.

"You called me a beast. You hurt my feelings."

"It was meant as a compliment." Xavier Paul yawned. "We've been civilized to death. We need the beast's seed now. You're a new man, Priest. Too bad you'll be dead."

"It was the way you said it." Priest sulked. "I didn't like that."

"Fair enough. Will you accept my apology?"

"I was mad. I wouldn't have said what I said—about queers and women—but you made me angry."

"Right. Why don't we drop the subject?"

"Look. You don't have to be so cold. We're friends. I want to be a friend. I'm a nice guy, but you shouldn't say things like that. I have a bad temper."

"I said, let's drop it."

"Damn you." Priest rose, palms on the car ceiling. He pushed off, twisting, backward. He dove. His shoulder struck Xavier Paul's shoulder. He heard the rear door-handle click. It opened.

"What is it?" Xavier Paul had shifted toward the door. "What do you want back here?"

"Are you getting out?" The door shut. The quick, defensive reaction had embarrassed Xavier Paul. "Are you afraid?"

"Your movements are very sudden. You've hurt me once already. I find your exuberance dangerous."

"No. You think I'm going to kill you. Huh? Is that it?"

"You've become very interested in killing. Like a new toy, isn't it?"

"Mmmm." Priest leaned back. They sat side to side, feet up. Then Priest put a testing on Xavier Paul's left biceps. "When I broke that guardsman's teeth, he was afraid. He was scared to death. There was nothing he could do, all screwed up like a woman getting laid. E-diet cramps. I had him. You should have seen the fear in his eyes."

"Don't enjoy it, Priest. Don't make it a habit."

"Why not? It's fun." His hand probed into the crook of Xavier Paul's elbow.

"Think you can take me?" The hand left furtively. "I'm a pretty old man."

"Sure. Even with my ankle like it is. Even if you're the biggest son of a bitch I ever saw. I'm strong."

"Are you?"

"Yes."

"You poor fool. Strong? You're a child. A sniveling infant." Xavier Paul began to laugh. "A lot could be done with you. But it's too late for that." Xavier Paul laughed again: a whinny, nasal and harsh.

"Stop it." The sound was sourceless. It disconcerted Priest.

Xavier Paul laughed.

"Stop it." Priest sat up, tried to cover the mouth with his palm. He couldn't find it. "Light a match."

"Why?"

"Now. Light it." Priest was frenzied. "Light it."

"I have only a few."

"Light it." Priest's hands stumbled, searching across Xavier Paul's lap. "Now. Now."

"Why?"

"Light it!" Priest shouted. "I want to see your face."

"There. Satisfied?" The igniting flash stayed on Priest's retinas. It starred his glance. "Well? What do you see?" Priest fingered the broken nose: a hutch of lumps. He parted Xavier Paul's beard, as though combing for vermin. He nodded. "Do you mind? I'd rather not burn my fingers." Xavier Paul blew the match out.

"I'm going crazy." Priest slapped the side of his own head: it was an uncompromising blow. Xavier Paul winced. "You know . . . I thought you were just a voice. I thought you weren't there. And sometimes I think Mary is here. And she isn't."

"Can't you tell from the stink?" Xavier Paul snorted. "God knows, you certainly baptized me with piss."

"Baptized?"

"Not that you smell too fragrant at the moment. My urine is more delicate. A kind of perfume." Xavier Paul pushed Priest back. "You can stop leaning on me, thanks. Now that your identity crisis is over."

"Do you use special water?"

"For my piss?" Xavier Paul laughed. "It's not the water— it's the excellent processing system."

"No. No. To baptize."

"Oh." Xavier Paul frowned. "Ordinary water is all right. If I bless it."

"We have water here." Priest rolled the window down. He swept one palm over the vinyl roof, rubbed the palm on Xavier Paul's cheek. "See."

"Yes—"

"Baptize me."

"Why? Because you've got nothing else to do this evening? Because you're bored? You just told me, didn't you, that you can't believe in God?"

"I never said that. I never said I didn't believe in God. I said it about the other world. I believe in God."

"You do? You've thought about it a lot?"

"Yes."

"I see. When? When was the last time you thought about God?"

"I—" Priest held his breath. He stalled. "Don't pressure me. Don't try to confuse me with words."

"I'm not. Do you believe in God?" Priest paused. "Well?"

"Mary does." Xavier Paul heard Priest's knuckles crack, a toy being wound. "She talks about God, when we're in the woods. About God's world; the things He made. I never said no."

"That's rather a lukewarm commitment, isn't it?"

"But . . . I never had someone to tell me about Jesus Christ. How was I supposed to know? Was I supposed to guess about it?"

"That's true. Yes." Xavier Paul was tempted: the final conversion, significance given to his slack ministry. Yet he knew Priest's cynicism. "Well . . . perhaps tomorrow."

"I want it now."

"You want." Xavier Paul became indignant. "You want. I'm tired of you wanting. I want to get some sleep."

Priest said nothing. His left hand traced the pistol's outline through rubber. This was a reflex already: Xavier Paul knew it comforted Priest. He prayed nonsensically, in patched formulas: his own sort of reflex. Something chattered beyond the window; the sound proliferated. A flock of bats exited through the roof. Priest's tongue prepared his lips. He said,

"Please."

"Please what?"

"Baptize me."

"Please? Are you being polite? Please pass the salt?"

"I'm asking you nice." Xavier Paul smiled at the darkness.

"I appreciate that. I know it must be difficult for you. But—" Xavier Paul covered Priest's hand with his own hand. "Listen to me. This is the most important thing I know. I have very little to look back on, less to hope for. This has been my comfort and peace for seventy years. Now—two days from my death—now I don't want to make my life seem cheap."

"I'm a beast, that's what you mean. You don't give the blood and the meat to a beast."

"Blood and meat?" Xavier had heard saliva in Priest's words. "This is my faith we're talking about. Not a menu. Not an act of cannibalism."

"I know."

"It's wine. Just a sip, not blood. And bread—not even real bread—thin wafers. Like pieces of paper. They have no taste. They stick in your throat."

"Uh-huh." He didn't think Priest believed him.

"Let me ask one question. Try to answer me honestly." He inhaled; he wanted sleep. "Jesus Christ was the Son of God; I told you that. He was sent to earth. He became man. He preached and performed wonderful miracles. He was put to death by men. His death was necessary; by his death, his sacrifice, our sins are forgiven. He rose again from the dead. This—the bare bones of it—this is what Christians believe. I explain it badly. But . . . my question is, can you believe in Jesus Christ? In some part, if not wholly."

"Yes."

"I see." Xavier Paul sighed. He remembered Priest's teeth. His brother, a monk, had once said, "I hunger for Jesus." But had anyone, he thought, ever hungered for Jesus as Priest hungered? "Can I ask another question?"

Priest shifted uneasily. "Yes."

"Are you sorry for your sins?"

"Sins?"

"Sins. Things you've done wrong."

"I told you. I told you. I know the word. But what are my sins?"

"You tell me."

"I don't know."

"Do you think you're perfect?"

"What is perfect?" Priest edged away. He was becoming bored, yet he wanted this thing, baptism. He wanted to make Xavier Paul surrender it. "I'm as good as any man. I don't see other men who are better."

"I'm not talking about other people. You killed two men, Priest."

"You said it wasn't wrong," Priest whined. They had argued this once already. "You said it was self-defense."

"Yes." Xavier Paul considered. "But you're glad you did it. You would do it again. You enjoyed it."

"That's wrong?"

"Yes."

"It's always wrong to enjoy anything, isn't it? That's what they say."

196

"I'm not talking about them. I'm talking about God. To God you're a proud, savage man. You have no penitence."

"So?"

"So—this you must understand. That you, Dominick Priest, are nothing. That your life is nothing. That before God your existence is meaningless. Meaningless, except that God sent His Son to die for you. You have sinned. You sin now."

"You don't sin, huh?"

"I do. I do. I know what I am." Xavier Paul became defensive; then he was infuriated. He found Priest's shoulder, shook the man by it. "Don't you tell me what I am. You aren't smart enough to know. You couldn't know in a million years."

Priest removed the hand gently. "I don't have a million years."

"No. No, you don't."

"So what can I do?" Priest was crafty: he had begun to understand the game. "Don't you want another Christian? Who will baptize me if you won't?"

"No one will." Xavier Paul hugged his own chest.

"You could do it. But you don't want to share. You want to be the last one."

"Do I?" Xavier Paul rubbed his forehead. "Do I?" he asked under his breath.

"I don't see. These things you tell me—my life has no meaning. Didn't you say that? Priest, in God's eyes your life is nothing. A rabbit's track in the spring snow." His voice rasped: an articulate sob. In one day he had learned intonations, vocal devices. "But I know that. How could I not know

197

it? Since I was born they've told me that. I don't know about your God, but when I killed a bee with my hands because it was stinging me to death—then they told me I didn't deserve to live. If that's what a Christian is—nothing . . . then we're all Christians here. And the mosquito is our God." He touched Xavier Paul's knee. "But you were the first man who told me to live. I thought you were different. Now—now, I'm not sure. I think the mosquito is your God, too."

"No. That's not true."

"You asked me if I liked you. Remember? I know why you asked."

"Why?"

"Because you don't like me. You wanted to ask it before I did. I know. I can feel it in my hair."

"In your hair?" Xavier Paul laughed: but Priest's judgment had been accurate and he was troubled.

"In my hair. Like when you rub a cat's back and the sparks come out."

"I see." Xavier Paul fondled his pipe. "You're right. I'll be honest. I can't like you—not until you stop frightening me. Instead I have a sort of reluctant admiration. Because of the fear. Look . . . you've got it wrong. I've explained it badly. You're nothing before God. That's easy enough to figure out. God is supreme if he is God. But you, Priest—I, Xavier Paul —we're each a special and personal creation. Beasts and fishes, but man alone was made in God's image. You bow to no one, flesh or graven image. And life is His gift. You don't throw it away."

"No? Not even if they come to kill you?"

"Not even. Not even then."

"I see." Priest tried whistling, but he had forgotten the mechanism.

"I am very taken with you, Priest." Xavier Paul was embarrassed. "Like is not a word we use for tigers. And you are a tiger."

"Will you put the water on me? Please?" Xavier Paul started: there were feminine tones now in Priest's voice, pleading, sensual. It was grotesque.

"I haven't done this in years. I don't remember all the words. I have a prayer book somewhere, but I can't read it in the dark."

"That doesn't matter. That's not a good reason."

Xavier Paul sighed. "It's a poor reason. Anyway I have no choice. If you understood my faith, you would guess that. I don't dare not baptize you. Not now, not with so little time left. You'll make a dinner of Christ, I know that. Suck the marrow from his bones, string your bow with his sinews. You'll never be a Christian. There isn't a chance in ten thousand . . . But I have no choice."

"Then do it."

"Come here."

"Watch—my neck."

Xavier Paul's left arm had scythed, a half circle in the darkness. It captured Priest's nape, settled there, forefinger and thumb each pinching flat an earlobe. He brought the unco-operative head down/against his ribs. Priest gasped. Xavier Paul adjusted the head, as though Priest's face gave light, and he was scanning the car floor by it. Priest began to squirm. Xavier Paul found nerve complexes in the neck, caused pain. Priest howled.

"Be still."

"I can't breathe. You're hurting me."

"Shut up." Xavier Paul hummed. "I'm trying to remember how it goes. You have no godparents, Priest. This is a lousy business."

"What?"

"Shut up. Lord forgive me." He smacked his lips, then made Priest's vertebrae crackle. He intoned. "Has this child been baptized already?"

"I'm not a child."

"Shut up, I said."

"Hey. Owww. Stop." Xavier Paul used the soft bottom of his fist. He pounded Priest's cranium above the neck, where it rose in a straight, undifferentiated plane.

"Shut up. I'm giving you the greatest gift there is. I don't like it, but I'm doing it." Priest groaned; he was afraid to resist. Xavier Paul hit him methodically. Priest skullcapped his head with one hand. "Great. Big. Stupid. Donkey. Ignorant. Undeserving. Dumb. Wretched." Xavier Paul wheezed. "Lord God, forgive us both. We are fools, apt inheritors of a dead world that was once Thy glory and Thy joy. Give this man the sacraments of baptism and unction, for he will surely die soon. Make the words I speak of some meaning. Lend efficacy to this act. Forgive me: I do this under extreme duress, Lord. You know my unwillingness. Yet, if it is Thy will, let this cup pass from me." He was silent. Priest ex-

200

amined his scalp. "Do you, Priest—do you, Dominick Priest, promise to obey God's will and his commandments?" Xavier Paul waited. "Say yes."

"Yes."

"Do you wish to be baptized?"

"You know I do."

"Yes."

"Yes."

"Do you promise to renounce the devil and all his works? The sins of the flesh."

"I don't—" Xavier Paul punched him, knuckles out now, above one ear. "Yes. Yes. Do you have to hit me?"

"It's part of the ceremony. Shut up." Xavier Paul hesitated. "Merciful God. Grant that this child, this man, be regenerate in Thee. As Christ died and rose again, so let him die and rise again. Grant him new life. Grant that he may have power and strength to triumph over the world, the flesh, and the devil. Through Jesus Christ our Lord." Xavier Paul lifted his right hand. Fingers dabbed in a small gutter above the car window. "I baptize you in the name of the Father and the Son and the Holy Ghost." Priest whimpered. Xavier Paul had used the sharp edge of his fingernail. "We receive this man into Christ's flock and do sign him with the sign of the cross, in token that hereafter he shall not be ashamed to confess the faith of Christ and . . . and to continue Christ's faithful servant and soldier to his life's end. Amen."

Xavier Paul unyoked him. Priest clapped palms over his

201

forehead. The sign was scored there in cruciform dents. He bled slightly. Xavier Paul's body had become slack beside him. Circulation returned: an inner, spangling light danced across the perfect darkness. Priest sat, hands in his lap. After several moments he said,

"Is that it?"

"Yes. God forgive me. You're a Christian."

"Light another match."

"Are you scared again?"

"No. Light another match."

Priest took the match, coddled its flame with a curving palm. He climbed over the front seat back. The rearview mirror swiveled down in its socket. Priest held the match under his chin: saw left profile, right profile. Xavier Paul shook his head; he smelled hair searing. The flame went out.

"You won't look any different."

"No?" Priest massaged his neck. "My head still hurts. You mean they did that to little children?" Xavier Paul said nothing. "Can I eat the meat and blood now?"

"Wine and bread."

"Yes. Wine and bread. Can I?"

"Tomorrow I'll confirm you. We'll have a first communion. I might as well go through with the whole thing."

"Not tonight?"

"Not tonight. I'm going to sleep now."

"You really socked me good. I think you enjoyed yourself."

"I wonder." Xavier Paul yawned. "Did I live until now

. . . all those useless years . . . did I live just to baptize you?"

"Maybe."

"I would be very disappointed." He yawned. "Very. Very disappointed."

IT WAS TEN O'CLOCK. They had been walking north since dawn. Thousands of white-tail deer waited in the wide Thruway valley. Their hoofs scuffed moths up. Many lay dispirited, heads doddery, anticipating sleep or death. Carcasses showed all states of decay: thin-snouted, clean skulls; mummified skulls as of papier-mâché; just dead eyes that stared, jellies still intact. Priest, now twenty yards ahead of Xavier Paul, shouldered deer aside. He struck at noses, flanks with his cane. Deer died under his harmless attack: sudden adrenalin exploded their hearts. His progress was awkward. The Thruway's double bed had been landscaped with high-bush blueberry shrubs. Their leaves had been stripped by the moths, stem tips pared down by the deer. Thick, low-branch stumps remained, palmate, hands of dead men reaching out of shallow graves. Priest walked with his insect mask open. There were active morning breezes. He was cheerful.

Priest had felt life in his ankle. The joint ached: bones seemed to settle in stages when he stepped, telescoping tubes. They had seen no other travelers on the Thruway. Priest sang. Deer folded their ears back/away from the raucous sound. The northbound lane was a tier above the south-bound lane, fifty feet of slope between. A small river meandered below. The trees were blasted. Only evergreens to his right, on the dynamited rock escarpment, still throve. His boots were tarred with caterpillar substance, feathered with moth wings, some wings yet alive, waving there. The moths seemed to die in special rendezvous, as snow lies within sunless hollows far into spring. Xavier Paul had been lagging for an hour: Priest was impatient. The old man's back had deteriorated. When they rested, Xavier Paul could not stand again without Priest's help. On hills he tried to hook with his cane, drawing up. His jaw was inclined; his shoulders bunched. Pain brimmed at the bowl edge of his hips. He balanced it as he walked. Yet twinges sloshed over, and often now he cried out involuntarily.

Priest had made a decision. He was exhilarated by it; he did not want then to think of Mary. He was too close. Already, through the valley gap, he saw familiar silhouettes: obverse faces of the mountain range just south of Bull's Hump. Priest turned toward Xavier Paul. The baptism had intrigued him. He did not understand its significance, but Xavier Paul had aged overnight, as though Priest had stolen life, had added it to his own great vitality. Priest walked back. He was in a hurry. Yet he was shrewd: he wanted the flesh and the blood. He waited as Xavier Paul approached with prudent strides. Priest grasped the tip of Xavier Paul's cane and pulled him along. He heard two wine bottles clank: the old man had refused, mistrusting wisely, when Priest offered to carry the heavier sack.

They walked in tandem for half an hour. Then the sky turned overcast with starlings. Their descent was breathtaking: the ground for a square quarter mile became gray/black, choppy. Capes, hoods appeared on the submissive deer. As Priest walked, the starlings ate from his boot tops: he felt ticklish pecks. Along the roadside bare tree branches were fully leafed—an abrupt, funereal summer. Priest laughed into the buffeting turbulence. Birds rode on Xavier Paul's cane, spiteful, flecked with buff and white. Yellow beaks snipped at the worms of his fingers when he moved them. Priest stared toward the river, and sounds around him, twitterings, purling, seemed the river's sound closer, in rapids. He could no longer hear Xavier Paul. Then the birds rose, an echelon two hundred yards wide, started by some joint instinct. They flew far north, landed, bodies compacting, flock compacting, smoke of a long firebreak sucked back to its source. Priest dropped Xavier Paul's cane.

He scrambled ahead. The Thruway had been walled in along its right shoulder. A sheer granite face began there, seventy feet high, extending north nearly two miles. A ten-foot fence lay along its steep upslope, as though sieving the earth. Priest clambered, on fingers and toes, hooking into the rusty wire angles. For several minutes he watched Xavier Paul, all perpendiculars, cane and legs, as he walked below. He did not see Priest, unable to crane upward. Priest heard his name echo on the granite face. He did not answer, but stared north. A corona of Bull's Hump, mauve, twenty miles distant, was eclipsed by the nearer summit of Eagle Peak. Across the river a bear lumbered, udderlike sags of flesh and fur jiggling under its body. The bear had gone crazy. It swiped brusquely, killing, maddened by a strange diet of venison, by the shiftless multitude that had destroyed its privacy. Deer panicked, heads up; fear was high in their nostrils. Priest drew Xavier Paul's prayer book out of his thigh pouch, then the .45. He sighted along its barrel. But the bear was too far away.

A last capsule nestled in the seam of his thigh pouch. Priest held it against the sun, between thumb and forefinger. Then he listened to it. He pinned the capsule between upper lip and nose. Wind charged his face. He felt urgency in his bladder. Northwest, across the river, a broad surge of mist appeared at the horizon. It was flat, plump as a comforter; it pulled down over the foothills, tucked ends into a wide valley. It sent out blunt fingers: white, but marbled underneath with brown streaks. It was ten miles away. Priest watched, curious. Then he said, no. He shook his head. He brought his arm back and hurled the capsule out/across the Thruway. Momentum nearly carried him over the bluff's edge. Priest huddled down on his knees. He laughed. He had decided not to die.

Xavier Paul waited for him. His hands trembled. He walked now with forearms rigid, outriggers for his spine. Priest talked to himself. Xavier Paul thought Priest was handsome; he had seen such a face once gnarled in a tree root: brown, Asiatic, ineluctable. Priest walked almost normally, cruel to the ankle. He stopped in front of Xavier Paul. He knocked caterpillars from the old man's shins with his cane. Xavier Paul steadied a hand on Priest's elbow.

"I'm slowing you down."

"Well, hurry up then."

"No. I can't. I have to rest. You go ahead, you have to see your family."

"Sit down now, and you won't get up again."

"I won't sit. I'll go over there. I'll lean against the rock wall."

"No." Priest heard the wine bottles kiss. "I'll help you. Lean on me."

"It makes no sense."

"Like this."

Priest nudged under his armpit. He insinuated a long right arm beneath the haversack, then around Xavier Paul's shoulder blades. Priest thought the old man had become shorter. He felt a tic jumping in the pectoral muscle against his cheek. Xavier Paul's left arm lolled on Priest's neck, fingers responseless. He matched the old man's stride in length, doubled its frequency. Priest's roughness exacerbated the pain, but his strength seemed helpful. Xavier Paul was surprised by his concern.

"There's a mist coming," Xavier Paul said. "Easy. Easy. Strange. I've never seen a mist come from the north. Not at this time of day. Not with so much wind."

"I saw it from up there. Stop dragging your big feet."

"Across the river. Just a little beyond here. That's where I was born. Small town called Tuxedo Park. Almost ninety years ago. Ninety in October." Priest grunted. "What things I've seen. The first man on the moon. The last man on earth."

"You haven't seen that. Not the last man on earth."

"I haven't?"

"No. I've made up my mind. In the night. I'm not dying. I threw my last pill away." Xavier Paul was silent. "Did you hear me?"

"Good."

"Good. Is that all you can say?"

"Good. It's enough."

"Are you mad at me?"

"Uh? Mad why?"

"When you put the water on me. I know—you did it because I was going to die, didn't you?"

"Perhaps."

"I didn't know then. I didn't try to cheat you."

"Forget about it. You can't give it back. Wait. Stop. It hurts me." Xavier Paul straightened his back in stages. "I didn't do it only because of that. I think I baptized you to spite God. He hasn't done much for me lately. Now He's stuck with you." Xavier Paul laughed circumspectly, neck set. Priest stared. Then he laughed too.

"When can I eat the blood and the flesh?"

"Wine and bread. Ha . . ." Xavier Paul laughed again. "And they used to talk about primitive Christians. The new Adam. Look on him, Lord. And what a Garden of Eden."

He gestured. Priest saw. There was a smart regiment of pines below the southbound lane, to his left. Fifty trees, sown ten each in five parallel rows. They made crazy perspectives. Seen head on, five composite trees; as Priest moved, they seemed to proliferate, a deck of cards fanning out.

209

Xavier Paul wiped his forehead. The sun neared its zenith: eleven-thirty, Priest judged. He was out of time. The mist continued to flood from the valley, over foothills, quite low, a gray husk. Priest chewed his lip. The starlings had come back, swarming to the south, calling peet-peet: it was a different sound; they did not land. An emaciated doe lurched upward. Priest had thought it was dead. The doe's eyes jiggled; it responded to some vivid fear, postponing death. The animal took three steps, then folded heavily, four legs splayed. A bone broke. And now other deer were moving reluctantly, slowly, in a driven saunter. Toward the south.

"Better go, Priest. It's late."

"Yes." But Priest hesitated.

"Be careful. They won't let you get away with it. They'll try to kill you."

"Let them. I've got the gun. I've got time. I know the woods." Priest watched deer; he frowned. "There's plenty of meat. There's a feast out there. I'll get fat. And Mary. I'll have more children." Xavier Paul's face went pale. "You knew all the time. You knew I would make up my mind."

"No. I didn't. But I knew this—when the time came, you wouldn't die. It's like holding your breath—you can't commit suicide that way. It's not possible: in the end you breathe. The body says, live. Good. Maybe there is a God after all."

"Maybe? What do you mean, maybe?"

"Maybe. Maybe." Then Xavier Paul shouted pain. "It's a disk. It's gone. I felt it go. Help. Help me, for God's sake. Help me to lie down."

"Maybe?" Priest laughed.

"Please. Let me brace myself on you. Please. I'm afraid to fall. I'm afraid of the pain. I can't move my legs."

Priest unshouldered the haversack: two wine bottles pushed through the bottom, thin nates. Xavier Paul groaned; he was terrified. He went down, backward on heel points; Priest braced with both arms under the long, clenching ramp of his back. He lay supine. Priest slid chunks of pavement rubble from beneath his hips. Xavier Paul crossed hands over his abdomen. Priest stood: he stared angrily toward the mist. Xavier Paul shaded his eyes. The muscles of his jaw appeared; his feet were perpendicular against their ankle joints. Deer trotted past. Priest knelt, placed a palm on the haversack. Xavier Paul whispered,

"This is as far as I go. This is where I end. Some pilgrimage. I would sit in that big church, afraid to make a cross. Not even two pieces of wood nailed together. It was days, months between prayers. Or maybe it was all a prayer. You know what I thought about for twenty years? Food. There were wild blueberries on the hill behind the church. I would crawl there at night. I felt my way across that field. On my belly. Yes. 'And dust shalt thou eat all the days of thy life.' Gladly, Lord. Gladly. Popping them into my mouth. I got to know the night animals. Shrews and moles; we shared the same table." He laughed. "When I was a child someone gave me a chocolate Jesus for Easter. Who would make such a thing? A chocolate Jesus. Where did I get it? My mouth is watering."

"You mean it doesn't work. The baptism." Priest spat.

211

"Eternal life—what a stupid thing. Who could believe it? And the power. You promised me power."

"Oh yes. Power. There's plenty of power. But where does it come from?" Chipmunks ran: perhaps two dozen in a ragged skirmish line. They hurdled Xavier Paul's chest. Rushing south.

Priest stood. "What is that mist? Is it mist?"

"God forgive me." Priest looked down. The old man's eyes were terrible. Sockets had welled full of liquid; in it, the blue pupils seemed dead, drowned. "God forgive me."

"God? Make up your mind."

"I'm sorry. I'm sorry." He wept.

"You make me sick." Priest walked away, ashamed for men. He yelled back at Xavier Paul. "Crying. Big bag of wind. I'm stronger than you are. I knew that all the time. I don't want to be stronger. I was always stronger. Stronger than my father. I didn't want it that way. I couldn't help it. And they smelled it on me. They hated me because of it. They ganged up on me."

"Yes." Xavier Paul turned his head. "I've been feeling sorry for myself."

"You're an asshole. You don't even believe in what you are."

"I have believed. I will believe again. You don't understand."

"I understand. You're an old woman."

"I shouldn't have said that to you. It was spiteful. I had a chance to witness—not, God knows, that you'll ever care two figs for Jesus Christ. A chance . . . and all the more reason

212

for that. For your cynicism. But I wanted a sign. I expected more than this." Xavier Paul felt feverish: he was afraid to shiver; he clenched fists. "What did I expect? What did you expect, Priest? Think, man. Have some compassion. In thirty years I haven't seen another Christian. They decimated us. A man locked in a dark room, alone, do you wonder if he doubts the sunlight? For two thousand years people have believed in Jesus Christ. What was I supposed to think—that it all ends in Paramus, New Jersey? That it all ends in me? Paramus. Can any good come out of Paramus?"

"Stupid God. Stupid old man. Fairy tales. You make me sick."

"I'll make the mass for you. The flesh and the blood." He untied thongs of the haversack. "Please let me."

"I don't want your mass. It smells of weakness. You're a woman. The blood is between your legs."

"Please. Forget what I've said. I'll make the mass." With one hand he slid the wine bottles from his haversack. Priest walked closer, curious. Xavier Paul removed a small tulip chalice, a paten, four wafers.

"I haven't got time. Give me those bottles. I'll make myself the mass." He reached down. Xavier Paul fell across the bottles. He howled with fear and pain. He hugged the wine to him. Priest laughed. "Old woman. When you're dead, who will make the masses? I will. Me. I will make all the religions. I will make the gods and their flesh and their blood."

"Priest." Xavier Paul looked at him. "You terrify me. I hope you die. I hope they kill you."

"Yes? You think I can't take your stupid bottles away?" He stamped his foot. Xavier Paul cringed. "Where is your God?"

"He's tired of us."

"Not of me. He's tired of you. Not of me. I'm alive."

"Priest. I know it—you can do anything you want with me. I'll have to trust you." He drew back. The two bottles lay side to side on the ground. "Will you let me make a mass? The way men have done it for two thousand years? I have doubted. You can't have faith without doubt. But God exists. He is teaching me now. At the last. Will you let me make the mass?"

"I'll give you until the mist comes down." He pointed. Fringes had reached the plain. "To the big oak. That will be your mass. My wife is waiting for me." Xavier Paul nodded.

"Thank you. It's enough. You must be a bridge between us. Between then and now. It's important. It seems very important." He leaned sideways.

And the bottles began to hum.

Xavier Paul said, "Ssssh." He was transfixed, hopeful. He listened for revelations; he thought it was a sign. The noise became shrill. He murmured. Instinctively the thumb knuckle of Xavier Paul's right hand struck his forehead, his breast. It stopped, the cross uncompleted. Priest was on all fours, brushing a space of crumbled pavement clear. Prone then, he shut his ear on the ground. Thunder was transmitted to him. Reluctantly Xavier Paul put his hand on the bottles: they were still at once. Priest knelt up, stared northwest. Sound was independent now of the earth's telegraphy.

Xavier Paul could hear it: a distant, stupendous drumming. Priest stood, and it was in the soles of his feet.

"An earthquake?" Xavier Paul asked. "The veil of the temple—"

"That mist—" Priest began.

"What? I can't see it."

"Fire. Big fire. But the sound—wait here."

"Wait." Xavier Paul repeated. "I'll wait."

Priest ran north on the Thruway bed, until his vision had flanked the stand of pines. He saw for two miles, northwest: across the river, across the brown/yellow plain, to the bank of mist, beyond to the gap between foothills. Something had dropped from the mist. A shadow that broadened swiftly, breasted the plain across its mile width. Priest thought, a flood. It approached in crescent shape, concave at center. He squinted, shading sun glare with two saluted hands. "No," he said aloud. "Deer. A million deer." The brush fire had gathered them for a radius of ten miles; wind had herded them south with the smoke. They stampeded: a tidal wave. In the few seconds Priest watched, they had covered a hundred yards. Big trees went over. Only stone outcroppings, islands now, surfaced. They were coming toward the Thruway.

Priest hurried back to Xavier Paul. The scrub underbrush teemed suddenly, crepitating, the snap/pop of kindled twigs. They raced beside him, through his legs, rolling, caroming, bouncing—chipmunks, rabbits, mice—ferreted from their tunnels by the long, penetrant vibration. Deer collided. Erratic breezes played the tremendous sound, blowing it near, muf-

215

fling it. Priest stopped. He stared back, for the sight had fascinated him. Dust arched up; it had obliterated the smoke. The vanguard formed out of a ghostly plasma. Color was erased: black and gray and white drove it ahead across the plain. They were less than a mile from the river. Backs rippled up, the herd rippled up, mounting shallow dips in the plain, a single great back, alive, invertebrate. I have five minutes, Priest thought.

"What is it?"

"Deer. Millions. Millions of them. God—you can't believe it. They're coming right at us. Up. Get up. We'll be trampled."

"I can't."

Xavier Paul turned over, as infants will, sliding one elbow under his ribs, an inclined plane, levering with his heels. Priest knelt: it seemed that Xavier Paul's spine was no longer continuous. A knot had erupted, just over his hips, thrust out through taut rubber. They were head to head, butting stags. Priest plunged fingers into Xavier Paul's armpits, heaved up in a double action, draping the old man's great slackness across his left shoulder. He staggered. Xavier Paul shrieked, then he gasped—from Priest's height, he had first seen the stampede. Its center flagged; mile-wide bull's horns pincered, closing. And there was no end: deer still seethed through the distant gap. Priest and Xavier Paul were vulnerable there. The rock face prevented retreat. Priest estimated the herd's speed. He could make out individual deer now. They were less than a thousand yards away. Priest saw the bear lumber just ahead of its massed prey. Deer headed

216

it, ran alongside, then the bear was enveloped. A raccoon knocked itself unconscious on Priest's shin. He tottered.

"My God. Oh, my sweet God. It can't be."

"The stream," Priest yelled. "The stream will stop them."

"Never. Nothing can stop that."

"Walk, damn it. I can't carry you like this. We've got to reach the trees."

"My wine."

"Forget the wine. Walk."

"No." And, despite grim pain, Xavier Paul thrashed his dead weight, made it capsize. He fell from Priest's shoulders.

"Stupid man. Stupid man. Get up." Xavier Paul had found the corkscrew.

"Go. Run, Priest. Go."

"Get up. Leave the wine."

"Go!"

Priest hauled him up, fingers wrenched under Xavier Paul's insect-shirt collar. It stretched. The old man ducked his chin, found Priest's thumb knuckle, chewed savagely down on it. Priest cursed: he kicked Xavier Paul in the chest. He wanted a bottle of wine, but he had waited too long. Now the churning surf was five hundred yards away. Priest gave up. He ran at it. The grove of pines stood between him and the deer, fifty yards ahead. His hearing obsolesced; he sensed thunder in the hollow chamber of his mouth. His diaphragm trembled sympathy. Footing was deceptive; it met his feet, dipped. They hit the river and exploded it over banks for a quarter mile, crushed water to fine mist. The momentum hesitated, then recovered. Priest could see terrorized muzzles as he ran. Their eyes did not guide, thrown high, blank. Breastbones strutted up; the winter forest of antlers crossed, recrossed its branches back through an infinite perspective. Lead deer misjudged a single stride and were overthrown. The reaching right arm of the tide had already embraced, lapped the pines. The semicircle closed on him. Priest was beaten ten yards from the first tree. He pulled out the .45.

Six shots bucked at his palm. They were soundless in the greater sound. Priest could not miss. The charge was perfectly contiguous: each crowding breast and throat seemed to have a thousand legs beneath/behind. He fired as he ran at right angles to the stampede, traversing aim ahead. The first deer was dead at the apex of a lovely, high bound; it finished the arc gracefully, cannon bones bowed under. Then it came apart, head snapped back and over its shoulder, just five yards from Priest's feet. Others crumpled, abruptly legless, falling crosswise, a crooked stile of bodies. Deer behind were hobbled by them. They somersaulted, antlers pronging into the soil. A live windrow accumulated, then the ranks adjusted and fallen deer were climbed, some minor elevation in the ground now, blood spurts punched out of flanks and necks. But their impetus had been checked momentarily and Priest was inside the stand of pines.

They died on the trunks, brained there, limbs shattered, unable to swerve against the irresistible, crowding pressure. The trees strained them; one animal out of ten passed through to stand confused, in a sheltered eddy on the grove's south face. Priest had shinnied up the first narrow bole. Ten feet above, he found the stump of an amputated branch. His instep folded over it. For more than an hour the stampede rushed under him. His tree thrilled with impacts. He heard the shush of their pelts against bark. Pines on the northwest perimeter were axed down: they leaned into the branch tops of trees behind them. But Priest saw nothing. Dust obliterated sky and earth. Particles drifted in his nostrils, shutting them. His tongue shaped clay balls. He spat, spat: he wheezed asthmatically, afraid of fainting. He tore off the hood and clapped it over his mouth. The sound deafened him. His ears began to bleed. Then they were gone.

Priest slithered down. He walked on carcasses: for twenty yards his feet did not touch the soil. Deer lay, tongues eaten in half; hoofs twitched, a nerve memory of the stampede. Flesh aprons, four feet high, six feet high, surrounded the pine grove. North, on the plain, tumuli rose where some obstacle, a fallen trunk, an old fence length, had gathered bodies, as boulders in a swift current will collect flotsam. The brush fire had scalped foothills now: it burned fitfully, cut off from wind and fuel. The river was dammed with corpses. It had begun to fill a broad lake below the Thruway roadbed. Here and there a deer, merely stunned, would right itself in sections, doddery. One large stag waited, half its antlers lopped off, head wrestled down by the unequal weight, as if listening to the earth. It panted: downcast, ashamed. Carrion birds flew apathetically overhead, spoiled by their great good fortune. Priest reloaded his .45.

The shred of black fabric had adhered to an antler. Priest picked it off. Fuzzy horn tickled his thumb pad, made him shiver involuntarily. Priest walked back in a straight line until he had found Xavier Paul's body. There were no familiar landmarks; he had passed this place several times already. Deer were heaped on the remains. Patiently Priest lugged the corpses off. Xavier Priest's skull had been driven into four inches of soil, face downward. The occiput was pulverized, flayed of scalp and hair, scooped out by hoofs. The ground was chalked with bone dust. The rib-cage grating had been picked clean: no bone was longer than an inch. It seemed the skeleton of a man long dead.

Priest knelt, interested, not repelled. There was a miniature glass bowl, a thick bottom fragment of the wine bottle. It lay within smashed pelvis flanges. Priest examined the bowl. Crimson liquid, nearly clotted, nearly dry, painted the shallow indentation. Priest wet his lips. Then he dabbed one forefinger in the bowl, touched forefinger tip to tongue. Perhaps it was blood, perhaps wine: he didn't know the taste. Priest stood and began walking north again.

HE KNEW THE TREE. Branches chaliced, set on one foot, an empty snifter. Debris of his tree house floored the branch shoulders. Three rungs, short plank lengths, had been nailed to the trunk, now almost absorbed by its bark. Below, the thin soil intimated roots, toes wriggled in a sock. The pond lay thirty yards beyond; it was fist-shaped with tributary forefinger poking under the bed of Route 206. Priest knelt to drink. Weeping willows dragged its surface. Young frogs darted to the mud, streamlined as pairs of pliers. Priest cleared the green algae, hands swimming apart; often he had cleared a space to drink there thirty-five years before. He sipped, nose and cheeks and forehead under, but his throat was roped with apprehension. He could not swallow. He gagged.

The sign said ENTERING NEW LOCH—SPEED LIMIT 30 MPH. Priest had been walking three hours, since dawn. It had begun to drizzle. Poison-ivy leaves on the roadside shone as though greased. His insect mask was fastened, a disguise. Clover Knoll bunched on the left; it enforced a bend in the highway. Sebastian Priest's home—the service station, the house, the barn—lay directly behind it. Parts of the road were detoured with stone rubble. The knollside had collapsed and there was a hollow in it now like that under an upraised arm, fleshy breast of rock below. Priest stripped the haversack off his shoulders. It was almost empty: the Book of Common Prayer, the crimsoned sliver of glass, a few mushrooms. He climbed down, stored it in a cement-lined culvert under the road. He touched the thigh pouch. Priest had seen no one as yet, and he was afraid.

The barn had burned. Its silo seemed a lit flare. Hot gases had accumulated there. The hemisphere cap was shredded: in flame shapes it held an image of the explosion. Sebastian Priest's house had caught. The roof had been trepanned by fire, then doused by sudden rain; black soot stalactites oozed down the walls. Priest had not entered the house in twenty years. Round upper windows, ocular, were boarded over, XXX, some child's naive representation of death. Priest crossed the asphalt yard. His father's pillbox service station, built of cement block during two summers, was unchanged, overhead garage door warped open. The two pumps had vanished. The empty holding tank had collapsed twenty feet underground—pumps, earth, cement island drawn into its vacuum. Priest looked down. The pump heads appeared above murky water, tilted forward, men dog-paddling. His parents had been buried between the house and the service station. Priest had marked the place with a low, unmortared stone wall. The ground was alive with surface water: the two grave blisters appeared to have risen, impetuous. Priest did not walk toward them.

Of nine window panes in the imitation Dutch door there

was one yet intact. Priest saw it when the English ivy moved, underleaves thumbed up by breezes: a reflection there, while the eight other squares were moronic, black. Priest uprooted chunks of asphalt; he pitched them. They missed, bouncing back, somewhat rubbery: one penetrated the service-station office. He stepped nearer: SEBASTIAN PRIEST, Prop. He tossed again, but with gangling follow-through, intentless because the result was certain and he could postpone it. The pane belonged to him: a last functional portion of his inheritance. One piece hit, tinked, cracked, but did not shatter the glass. Priest sensed that his throwing was impersonal, perhaps a coward's way. He came close. A piece of shale, wedge-shaped like a Stone Age biface tool, lay on the brick planter. Priest handled it, discovered its balance. He opened his mask. Drizzle had glazed the pane, but he saw parts of brow ridge and eye and nose before its glass broke. A single bird, blue/white, afraid, leaped from the eave. It rose in an exact perpendicular, then soared through the mist. Priest walked away.

Mary's house, his home, was two hundred yards north, set on a slope well back from Route 206. Priest stopped. He tore off his thigh pouch flap. Then he set the .45 on its muzzle, butt upward. He hurried. He heard the noise of work. A heavy stone clattered against other stones. There were ten women on his long, downslanting front lawn. They were naked. He knew several: members of the New Loch Lesbian Commune. They hoed with fingertips lazily, sifting; movements were overelaborate and sensuous. One hauled rocks low, in a sling of embracing arms, held against the uptilt of

223

her pelvis. Their bodies were reddish, the skin caked with clay to discourage insects. Priest stepped forward. Logs of his front gate came apart when he pushed, stale bread loaves. His hands shook: the women worried him. They didn't belong here; he knew Mary would not have allowed it. A few watched him, hardly aware. They stared at places where Priest had been long after he had moved ahead, walking up/ toward the house. He counted six whole graves. Four were as yet incomplete.

The broad front porch had sagged. Its roof seemed to levitate, Corinthian pillars six inches now above the planking. It was a large house, fifteen rooms, but they had closed the upper story. The roof was square, with a false widow's walk around it. Priest began to stride faster. Curtains in the dining room were parted at an edge. Someone had seen him. A door opened and shut inside. Priest ran, off the path now, to his left, for Mary used the side door near the kitchen. Priest jerked back his hood, patted his face, raking fingertips through clotted forelock. He stopped, arms wide to hug. For some reason he thought the burlap shift, the pail covered with rags, were Mary and the child. It was foolish: an infant could not stand alone, and Mary's shift hung on a line three feet off the ground. But he had been running, and his eyesight, distorted, had superimposed expectation on reality. His arms dropped. The front door opened. Priest, at the left corner of the porch, swerved around.

It was Ogilvy; behind him, in the doorway, a junior guardsman named Mason. Ogilvy blurted, with adept fingering, into Mason's left forearm. They were disconcerted;

Priest had surprised them. Green guards uniforms were tattered, moist with earth at the knees. Mason's arms came out of his elbow pits, and the sleeves dangled behind, vestigial limbs. Priest trotted parallel to the porch railing. Ogilvy halted him, both hands up, at the stoop. Mason unholstered his stun can; he manipulated it at arm's length, crouching, eye along the cross-hair aimer. Priest opened his palms. He was submissive, cautious. The porch flooring grunted under Ogilvy. His face was pear-shaped, upper lip beaked out: the jowls were blue, heavy as bean bags, their dead saliva glands packed with infected gravel. He was thin: his insect-suit crotch made a deep Y to the points of his pelvis. Yet there were selected fats, toneless, stored by erratic hormones: above the pubis, in the buttocks; big lobes of tissue under his armpits. He grinned at Priest, but backed away from the landing.

"Where is my wife?" Priest trapped the sound; mouthed. By chance he became a ventriloquist then, and his last word was murmured from the porch cornice, ". . . wife?"

"Don't come any closer, Priest."

"Where is she?"

"Home to die, Priest?" Ogilvy smiled. Mason edged away from the steps. He lapped one leg over the porch rail, stun can alert, flanking Priest.

"Answer me, please. For God's sake."

"We're a little surprised. After all, we didn't expect you home. How did you get out? Escape? Did you kill someone?"

"They let everybody out. Is she in there? Is she in the house?"

225

"Well, no. Mary didn't expect you either. Can't blame her." Ogilvy put thumbs under his puckered armpits. "You've been an absentee husband."

"Where—tell me where she is."

"Mason. Show Priest where his wife is." Mason started, eyes aghast.

"Not alone. You come with me, Ogilvy. I don't like this guy. He's an animal."

"Sure. I wouldn't miss it. I want Priest to see his wife and child."

"My child?" Priest's mouth yawned. "My child—"

Ogilvy gestured. Priest went back, nodding, amenable. Ogilvy was astonished at the reach of his arms. From drooped shoulder caps they extended below the knee, fingertips touching at left thigh pouch. The man had been defeated: Ogilvy felt an exciting pity; it titillated him. "Ape," he said. Priest did not answer. The drizzle had snowed itself in white globules on Priest's greasy hair and beard: he seemed hoary, old. Ogilvy thought, but could not recall Priest's age. Mason jumped down from the porch rail. He led them at five yards, stun nozzle set on DISTANCE. Halfway to the gate they turned right, into the weed shambles. Mason, light and agile, did not appear to depress the damp, three-foot-tall nap of chess and barnyard grass and thistle when he stepped over it. A few women craned to watch them. One pointed, then forgot her purpose, stared at the pointing forefinger, puzzled by it. Priest's legs sickled: he was distressed—why would Mary be here, in the grass? Mason waved the stun can in loops, as if hurling it over his

226

shoulder. Then he leaped. He waited for them. Priest could not see what he had jumped across. He came nearer.

It was a grave. Mary lay in it, a strange infant clutched high against her shoulder. She had been dead perhaps twelve hours. Her left breast jutted, nipple purplish, between the baby's triangular heels. One palm rested at the small of its back. Her sharp features were slurred kissing into the child's side. Brown hair, carded tight by a rusty barrette, spread up the grave wall. Her buttocks lolled in a turgid puddle. Priest saw her feet, and in the sodden clay he saw one clear print—toes, arch, heel—the end of Mary's spoor. He stared, tongue out. Then Priest began to applaud. He made big clopping sounds in his palms, anguished. He was fully insane. He bellowed.

The sound was terrific. Mason winced. Priest anchored both heels in the earth, bellowed again, fists on kneecaps, pupils rolling up. It was a shout of triumph. The women trembled, afraid. They came together in groups, yanking at their fingers, their nipples. Ogilvy kicked Priest. He fell, curled, at the grave's edge. Mason stepped closer; he aimed the stun can at Priest's head. Ogilvy grinned. Priest began to grunt, Hmmmm-hmm, clearing his throat, ruminative. He dropped into the grave. There was scarcely room for his feet and they soiled her white calves. He knelt. Mary's breasts were fuller than he could remember. He wet fingers, touched them. The carotid artery in her throat was blue, sclerotic. The finger traced it from collarbone to ear lobe. Priest stripped off his insect-suit shirt. He shrouded her privates and breasts, the baby's buttocks.

Its small head would not turn toward him. Priest was gentle, afraid he might snap the neck. Mosquitoes settled over his back. Mason signaled, getting Ogilvy's attention. He shook the stun can. Ogilvy mouthed, Not yet. He was interested. Priest bent close, cheek to cheek with Mary, blowing dirt away. The baby's sparse hair stirred. A fetid, sour odor rose: Priest frowned; he was embarrassed for his wife. He examined the infant's eye, its nose; he thumbed the long cheekbone. The skull structure was prominent, threatening its skin. Priest smiled. The child seemed ugly. He heard a ticking. The capsule had landed on Mary's stomach, on his insect-suit shirt. Priest looked up. Ogilvy's fingers were outstretched, completing the toss. Mason had relaxed, on his haunches now. Priest's ankles were hobbled by Mary's body; he couldn't leap. As if curious, Priest picked up the capsule. And the fingers of his left hand worked down, along his thigh, to the .45.

"Swallow it," Ogilvy mouthed. "She's dead. Now it's your turn. Be a good boy and we'll bury you with her."

Priest ground his teeth. He did it impassively, lips drawn away. The sound was of ratchets, very loud. It revolted Ogilvy; gooseflesh rose along his nape. Enamel splinters broke off. Priest stared at the capsule.

"Swallow it. Now." Priest ground his teeth: dowels working in wood. "Stun him, damn it. Stun him."

The bullet split Mason's chin. Its report clapped through trees, was echoed from Bull's Hump. One woman fell, huddling. Mason swallowed, swallowed, prostrate now, kicked back ten feet. But the bullet had passed through his throat,

228

out. He blew a spume of aerated blood up in laconic whooshes. He hadn't seen the gun. Mason wondered what was killing him.

Ogilvy got his stun can out. Priest didn't try to kill him. He was already expert, using finesse. He meant to hit the arm, but shot just high. Ogilvy said, No. The bullet jostled him sideways, imbedding near his armpit. Priest leaped from the grave, unnaturally low, no more than two feet above the earth; he ran on all fours. Ogilvy limped in a circle, hand over heart, swearing to God. Priest's full weight hung on him, brought him down.

Ogilvy chatted aloud. He bared his throat when Priest touched it. He accepted death; he helped Priest's hands. Priest straddled him. He felt Ogilvy's rib cage swelling, subsiding deep in his groin. Blood welled to brim the armpit. Priest paused; he was thoughtful. He saw the white, freckly skin there, a fowl's breast. Priest peeled Ogilvy's biceps, working the green material down. Ogilvy did not resist. Momentarily, foolishly, he thought of first aid. Priest levered one palm under Ogilvy's chin, settled belly to belly on him, comfortable. As the women watched, those who would be the ten Eves of Priest, he ate Ogilvy's arm to the sweet flesh around its bone.

EPILOGUE

GREAT SUSURRATION: deerskin shuffled on stone. Oscar closed his eyes. The sound, repeated in ten thousand feet, was tidal, digestive. It elided broken phrases of the liturgy. A gully was worn along the center aisle; in mass and in persistence the deerskin had been a solvent of granite. The organist began again. Oscar heard chirps from the treadmill bellows outside, where three novice doms walked uphill, uphill. Oscar stared overhead. Peppery incense hazed the pillar capitals, triangles, each with flat surface enough for a dozen men to stand. All things—clerestory windows, pews, the font—were arrowheaded, recapitulating the cathedral's form, points aimed at an abstract image of Priest behind the altar. Under his severed arm, the mouths of a feeding world crowded, flowers: tulips cupped, daffodils, tongue-out impertinence of calla lilies. It was twilight. Two men backed away from the communion rail. Oscar knelt beside Eleanor.

The mortars were silent now. A dom heaved his censer. Oscar's eyes ran, but this was the third day, and a gamy stench had pervaded the cathedral apse. Blue flies breaded a chunk of meat; it quivered with their clung weight. Oscar reverenced himself: forefinger nail cut three times over the biceps of his left arm. He muttered the responses and heard Eleanor. She was too loud, self-conscious. She worried him. Her moccasin tips tattooed the floor. The mortar shot had been a disappointment. She was bitter; she blamed him. Eleanor nibbled around her mouth, gnawing the red lip grease permitted there only on feast days. Her teeth were carmined by it, cruel. She stared toward the altar. Seated opposite each other, two doms worked a treadle: it rotated the fat glass caldron of blood, swirling, inhibiting coagulation. Centrifugalization had crusted it red. Eleanor glanced left, elbowed Oscar. She meant to enjoy herself.

The first dom approached. He wore a sacramental mask: gilt plastic, wire mesh at eyes and nose and mouth. His head had been shaved; a black rubber skullcap fit over it. The left arm, red-sleeved, red-gloved, extended between the flaps of his robe. Eleanor cupped her palms. With thumb and forefinger, particular, the dom chose a sliver of meat from his bronze paten. Muted through the wire mesh, "Come and feed at my arm. I have given my flesh for you." Eleanor replied, "I accept this gift of grace and I am full of thanks." Eleanor's face was muzzled in her palms. She appeared to linger there, snuffling, rooting. As Oscar's hands went up to receive, he glimpsed the profile of Eleanor's throat, rippling down, a snake in motion. She shivered, perhaps with delight, perhaps with revulsion. Oscar felt the morsel between ring and middle fingers of his left hand. It seemed warm. Oscar saw that his share of the sacrifice was stringy. Glossed sinews, a fine paintbrush, daubed tinges of blood on his palm. Oscar responded. He ate. Then, as ceremony required, he sucked the tips of all ten fingers.

Someone had begun to retch. Desperate barking reverberated from the high vaults. It was a woman's noise, but Oscar could not see along the rail. Two guards hurried left, just behind him. Oscar was sympathetic, yet embarrassed, disdainful: women did not belong at the altar. A second dom neared Eleanor. He agitated the cup gently; stirred it with a long spoon after each feeding. Oscar watched Eleanor's tongue. It poked in recondite crevices of her mouth, under the upper lip, tasting man. Eleanor would not retch. Oscar faced away. He read the triangular apse windows: Priest rebuking the Ecologists; St. Mary and St. Xavier in prayer. HE MADE MAN LORD AGAIN OVER ALL THINGS OF THE EARTH. There was no historical authority for the windows. Priest, Oscar thought, had been a stupid man; stupidity had been the source of his power.

Eleanor nudged him. Oscar held the cup's stem. Its rim adhered to his lips. The sacrifice was in a degenerate state; the bowl had accumulated a gluey sediment. Oscar swallowed: the salt taste was not unpleasant, surprising him again. Oscar blotted his lips on the red armband embroidered seventeen years before by his mother, not washed in seventeen years. He stood.

They left together. Eleanor walked clumsily, arm under Oscar's arm; fingertips tested the mechanism of his biceps. She seemed drunk. She smiled; murmured a question, answered it herself. Unseen in a loft above, choirs began to sing the hymn of Priest's triumph. "Rejoice, rejoice today./

235

We have shared the glorious feast./ Great Priest's arm is safe within us;/ We are strong in his huge strength./ We are men again today./ We are men again today." Eleanor hummed along. She was pensive, but cheerful, no longer downcast. Oscar wondered: she is intelligent, she must know the story can't be true. And yet, he thought, it is true enough: man was meant to live and life will be celebrated. Life cannot be denied. Leo passed, entering with his two wives. He didn't see Oscar. Hands were clapped, in an anticipation of reverence, across his heavy bosom. Oscar put coins on a plate near the door.

The sun set, bisected at crater's rim. Diffuse rays seemed to erode the wall. Some birds had returned, cautious, edgy. An evening wind freshened: branches of tall oaks conducted the sky with great panache. Oscar paused on the cathedral steps. He felt fine. The smell of cordite had faded. Disposable earplugs were scattered over the stairway, spent cartridges. Eleanor jerked her braid: jaws came open as though tormented by a metal bit. Oscar admired her body. He belched, and the taste of man, not so very different, after all, from the taste of other animals, returned to his throat.

"What are you thinking now?"

"Cannibals or suicides," he said. "One or the other."

"What?" Eleanor frowned. His soberness irritated her.

"Shakespeare was wrong: there are only two ages of man. Childhood and senility. Savage youth or a self-hating, self-destructive civilization. In between, a few moments—no more, a few—when the balance is held, when he is a god."

236

"Shakespeare?" She didn't ask; she didn't want to know. "You read too much."

"Perhaps." He smiled. "Did you like it, Eleanor?"

"What?"

"The meat."

"Yes. I did. I did."

"Your teeth are so big, dear." He leaned close to bite her earlobe. Eleanor evaded him. "It's good, I guess. Good to know how one tastes. Self-knowledge. Self-knowledge." He started down the steps, aware that his voice had become shrill. Late communicants passed; some heads turned. "When we're through eating others, then we'll eat ourselves. Again. Like hoop snakes. That's what you see here: the birth of death. Another birth of death. What a sorry species."

"Don't spoil it for me." Eleanor ran to catch up with him. "You always do this."

"The reprisals will come. Not now. Not until we're long dead. The soul of man has secret teeth—it'll gnaw a way out. Cancer. Guilt."

"Shut up. Stop talking so loud."

Oscar didn't see him. The young father was engrossed. He wore lederhosen; a long peacock feather bobbed above his deerskin cap. The family posed around a statue of St. Xavier: mother, small sons hugging each a knee. Their set smiles quivered with long exposure. The young father paced off distance, counting aloud, toe exactly behind heel. One eye was shut, one eye full against the box-camera lens, the feather curving down, advisory.

His heel pinched Oscar's small toe against rough gravel.

Oscar gasped. His elbow struck, shoving; the movement was immediate and honest, an answer to pain. Oscar heard the sigh. He felt shapes of bone under the rib cage. The young man turned, fist over kidney. He blinked. The feather was apologetic. And Oscar shoved again, elbow honed, point forward, under the solar plexus. In a joined glance they understood that this was inexcusable, no reflex. He held his camera up. He was afraid of Oscar.

"Stupid jackass. Why don't you watch where you're going?"

"Sorry." The young father retreated. His camera framed Oscar. Eleanor watched the family: their smiles had been refurbished by concern, idiotic now, wide.

"I ought to break your head."

"I said I was sorry."

"Oscar. We're late. Leave him alone."

She drew her husband away. He acted reluctance. The young man signaled a prudent obscenity inside his hands. Oscar could not see, and the young man went, vindicated, to his family. Oscar and Eleanor walked along the rim, toward the colossal statue of Priest in Crater Plaza. Oscar's arm had tautened: Eleanor's thumb could make no impression on its muscle. They stood aside. One of the big tractors ascended a precipitous incline from the crater floor. Its twelve hooks had been retracted. They were caught in brackets on the chassis. The operator yelled conversation to his four hook men. They slugged from flasks, laughing, apparently tired. In Crater Plaza sweepers broomed the cobblestones. Double file, a primary-school tour waited. Two concessionaires secured a

238

metal grating across their stand. Oscar sat on the fountain lip.

Eleanor watched him. Oscar's midriff was smug, concave. Arms against his chest forced the pectorals out. He removed one moccasin, examined his instep, inventoried toes. There was no mark. Eleanor smiled. Water trickled out of the copper vein in Priest's half arm. She dabbled fingers. The statue's face, patinaed, a yard broad, was inclined exactly toward her. Eleanor felt unease. She explored the face. Its structures—jaw and cheekbone and brow ridge—were fiercely planar, indomitable, male. But she had always known that. In twilight the eyes were not scrutable; shadows had cluttered under their bronze lids.

Eleanor stood. She wiped her hand. She walked left until she found it. In the profile: Priest's austere mouth had parted, perhaps had only anticipated parting. But Eleanor saw compassion there and evidence of a smile. Priest had loved all men. Universal love: love for Eleanor. She was at peace and glad.

"Stupid jerk," Oscar said. "Did you see the look on his face?"

"I saw. He was afraid of you." She grinned. "That's what you mean, isn't it?"

"Afraid?" Oscar shrugged. "He was just stupid."

"He was afraid of you."

"I don't think so."

"Why not? You can be very tough. I'm even afraid of you sometimes." She grinned again.

"All right. Don't make fun, Eleanor. We're all children. I have my little weaknesses. These are primitive times—"

"Oscar. Please. Not now."

"What?"

"Don't lecture. I'm hungry. Let's go get something to eat."

"Yes?" He smiled. He kissed her lips. "Priest, yes. Let's go. I could eat a horse."